union
square
kids

NEW YORK

NION SQUARE KIDS and the distinctive Union Square Kids logo are
trademarks of Union Square & Co., LLC.

on Square & Co., LLC, is a subsidiary of Sterling Publishing Co., Inc.

ISBN: 978-1-4549-4625-0

Library of Congress Control Number: 2022930799

or information about custom editions, special sales, and premium
purchases, please contact specialsales@unionsquareandco.com.

Printed in the United States of America

Lot #:
2 4 6 8 10 9 7 5 3 1

07/22

unionsquareandco.com

ll photos courtesy of Lücastoothé Enterprises, Inc., except the
ollowing: Library of Congress: 328 (city), 331 (mustache);
J.S. Fish and Wildlife Service/National Archives: iii, 328 (ferret);
lberto Bigoni/Unsplash: iii (mustache); Alfredo1666/courtesy of
Wikimedia Commons: iii (cave)

QUEST KI
and the DRAGON PANTS of G

original WORDS *and* DRAWINGS *by*
NED

RESTORED, TRANSLATED, *and* EDITED
J.B. LÜCASTOOTHÉ

additional WORDS *and* DRAWINGS *by*
MARK LEIKNES

union
square
kids

Foreword

My own journey began in the summer of 1947 while on holiday with my ferret Oscar. I was exploring the caves along the Rhine River in northern Switzerland when I made a discovery that would change my life forever.

Oscar and myself, Switzerland, June 1947

I unearthed an ancient text detailing a world only remembered in myth and fairy tale. A world of wizards, elves, trolls, and dragons. A world described in such a vivid manner that neither Oscar nor I could distinguish it from fact or fiction. I leave it up to you and your ferret to decide for yourselves.

I have spent the last seventy years restoring this rare collection of works, the first of which you now hold in your hands. But let the reader be forewarned! What follows is **NOT** for the faint of heart. If peril, adventure, and death are subjects that you're just not all that into, I beg of you to abandon this text and turn back now!

Still here? Then, without further ado, let us buckle up and begin the tale of brave Ned and his questing friends!

—J.B. Lücastoothé

J.B. LÜCASTOOTHÉ, *curator*
of the QUEST KIDS *manuscripts*

CHAPTER 1

Not all of our **QUESTS** will involve us stealing pants off dragons. I just want to make that perfectly clear right up front. **DEPANTSING** large animals is super dangerous and not the sort of thing we go about all willy-nilly.

1

Okay, that was really the only other time.
Besides, dragons are **BAD** and don't deserve
pants. This one forced an entire mountain
village to smelt gold into thread and sew
it into giant sparkly **SWEATPANTS.**

Daddy, my fingers hurt from **SEWING GOLD** all day.

Sew the shiny pants, sweet child, so we shan't be **BURNT LIKE TOAST.**

HOLD UP, I'm getting way ahead of myself. You don't even know who I am. This is **ME...**

I go on adventures, or **QUESTS**, if you will. Then I write about them in this super helpful field guide — that way new questers can learn just what it takes to mount a successful quest! These are my friends, the **QUEST KIDS!**

TERRA is an elf. She's 700 years old, but looks like she's 11. Maybe 11 is 700 in **ELF YEARS**, I don't know. But being so much older than us might be why she is so much smarter than us, too.

BOULDER is a rock troll. Normally, rock trolls soullessly squash folks into assorted jams, but Boulder is **REALLY NICE!** That could be why his terrifying rock troll parents abandoned him. But we don't talk about that :..(He's also a fabulous cook, by the way.

GiL is my best friend. We both hail from the village of Hamhaven and have known each other since we were little. Gil was a star pupil of Gazimar the Great and studying to be a full-on wizard until the day his teacher **VANISHED.** All that was left was his beard, which Gil wears in his honor.

ASH is our dog, well, pig, well, thing. Okay, so we don't know what Ash is, but we do know that he's protective, loyal, and smells not amazing. Think old eggs set ablaze by the midday sun, then doused with **FLAMING SAUERKRAUT.** Yeah, it's bad.

As for **MYSELF**, like Terra, I look 11 years old, but unlike Terra, I actually am 11 years old. I'm also an orphan like Boulder — my parents disappeared the same night Gil's teacher did. Gil and I set out on a quest of our own to find out what happened to them. Along the way, we met Terra, Boulder, and Ash. But when **OUR** quest grew cold, we decided to take

on **OTHER PEOPLE'S** quests to make a living.
Which brings us back to **THIS** quest right here.
Our little group was passing through town
and had just split up to gather some supplies.
It was then that the villagers made their
FORMAL QUESTING OFFER to me.

Wilt thou
bravest of knights
bringeth back
thine dragon-sized
SPARKLY PANTS?

thumbs
up

Well, maybe not so much to me, as it was to this
couple of highly skilled knights. But luckily, I just
happened to overhear everything. So I quickly

hooked back up with my friends and convinced them that we should secretly tag along. Which ended up being sort of a **GOOD THING.**

Except, not so much for the Knights.

HIGHLY SKILLED KNIGHts
(recently dragon-roasted)

I mean, don't get me wrong, we'd love to be everyone's **FIRST** choice. But it's hard getting hired for quests when you're a **KID,** or look like a **KID,** or are a **KID** wearing a fake beard, or are a terrifying rock troll who also happens to be a **KID.** And I guess calling ourselves the Quest **KIDS** probably isn't helping our case much, either.

8

But all that will change once we complete our **FIRST QUEST!**

PuZZLeD READeR

(maybe not-so-helpful field guide)

Wait, you wrote a book about questing, but you've never **FINISHED** a quest?

While it may technically be true that we've never **FINISHED** an actual quest, let the record show that we've **ATTEMPTED** many.

QUEST ATTEMPT #**1**: SLOW StaRT

point

TAR PiT

And it's also somewhat true that no one has ever **HIRED** us to quest. But that hasn't stopped us from questing for them anyway.

QUEST ATTEMPT #2: WHOOPS.

Sure, our attempts can go terribly **WRONG** or even **NOWHERE** at all. But in spite of this, we keep trying over, and over, and **OVER** again.

Cuz you can't be a success in life until you **FAIL FIRST.** And now that we've gotten all that failure out of the way, we can really start concentrating on the **SUCCESS** part!

QUEST ATTEMPT #6: DRAGON US DOWN!

Okay, now everyone pull **TOGETHER** on the count of three...

CHAPTER 2

So my friends might be under the impression that our quest is more of a rescue mission than it actually is. While I'm **SUPER KEYED-IN** on redistributing these giant golden trousers, they're **ULTRA-FOCUSED** on finding Chubberstone Furballia the Third, a fictional cat I told them the dragon stole. I guess I just felt like I had to spice things up to get them to come along. Especially after our last depantsing ended so badly.

Look, as quest leader, sometimes you need to tell a little white lie to **GREASE** the questing wheels. You know, get things moving. This could be considered "wrong" if your group is not up to the challenge. But in our case, I **KNOW** we can do these things.

ReCeNT QUEST ATTEMPTS

#1: SLOW START

#2: WHOOPS

#3: MOMMY iSSUES

#4: WEATHER WE SHOULD?

#5: NOT OUR TIME

Okay, technically we have **NOT** been able to do these things. But we still need to get out there and try. And if that means **FABRICATING FELINES** with long and overly specific names for us to save, so be it.

Disturbing the slumbers of things that can heave **WHITE-HOT FLAME** upon you is generally something I try to avoid. However, now that the beast is awake, I know what you must be thinking. Why not just **SLAY** it? Hmm, that's a great question. Why don't you ask these guys?

EXTRA CRISPY KNIGHTs
(really into slaying)

Oh wait, you can't, cuz they're **DEAD.** 💀
No, slaying things is senseless and dangerous.
I don't even own a sword. Those things are
WAY SHARP! Therefore, when trouble rears its
ugly head, it's best to pursue one of two
options. **(A) RUN** or **(B) HIDE.**

OPTION A

Trip

snap

There's also a common misconception that when a friend trips while facing mortal danger you should go back for them. Let's call that option **(C) SAVE.** This really depends on the friend in danger and the amount of danger. If the danger would definitely **PANCAKE YOU** but only make your friend uncomfortable, then stick to option A or B.

Being **MMOR (M**ostly **M**ade **O**f **R**ocks) makes Boulder slightly more durable than pretty much anyone else ever. I was hoping the dragon might stumble over the **HARD-HEAVY-THING** in its path and perhaps twist an ankle. But, sadly, the beast just sidesteps Boulder and continues after us.

Never lead a dragon back to the village after a quest goes bad. That's Questing 101, plain and simple. Any good quester will tell you that it never ends well. We totally learned that right away after **QUEST ATTEMPT 2.**

If you really stop to think about it, this whole thing is kinda the **VILLAGERS' FAULT.** I mean, why'd they hire someone to steal dragon pants anyway? Did they not think their village would be the **FIRST PLACE** the dragon would look?

And, assuming the dragon doesn't burn down your village in **REVENGE**, it's definitely going to make you spend another year **SMELTING** and **SEWING** a new pair of dragon sweatpants. Bad form, oppressed mountain villagers, bad form.

It does not seem likely that we will survive this quest, and neither will the mountain village for that matter. What can it hurt to see if this giant **BEDAZZLE-PANTED BEAST** can be reasoned with? So let us try the not-so-frequented **FOURTH OPTION.**

WHY are you doing this?

You tried to steal my **PANTS!**

Sorry, thought that was obvious.

No, why'd you force these poor villagers to make gold sweatpants?

Cuz they **STOLE MY GOLD!**

← point

Wait, what?!

It was just a **TINY** bit.

Which is why I **DiDN'T** burn your **TiNY** village to the ground! Instead, I was nice and thought of a punishment to make you hate gold so much you wouldn't steal mine again. Also, I really wanted some **LOUNGEWEAR.** Oh well, so much for that. Time to

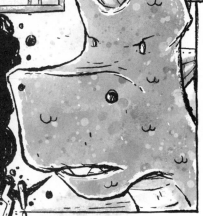

TORCH THINGS!

WAiT!

WHAT ABOUT A GOLD SWEATSHiRT?!

I'm listening.

Seems **SiLLY** to lie around **ALL DAY** in only sweatpants!

You should have a shiny new gold **SWEATSHiRT** to go with them!

Would it have a hood?

Would you like a hood?

Not really.

Then it would not.

Could it zip up in the front?

Um...sure?

CHAPTER 3

We had not been roasted alive today. A huge win! We were also hired for our very first **OFFICIAL QUEST.** Another awesome thing! Sure, leading a dragon back to the village could have repeated the failure of Quest Attempt 2, but it didn't. So that makes me **A HERO!**

Okay, the villager has a point. Yes, in one year's time, their entire village will most assuredly become a **SMOLDERING PILE** of ash and ruin. But they do have a year, and a lot can happen in a year.

It took a **WHOLE YEAR** to smelt and sew the gold into **SWEATPANTS!** We'd need all the gold **TODAY** to even have a chance!

Point

Awww!

When I promised a super-soft zip-up golden track jacket to the dragon, I was just saying **ANYTHING** to survive. I had no idea if it was even possible. I figured the **HOW** of it all would just sort of work itself out.

Pony

Hey, um, just **FYI**, this old pile of rags is laughing.

he he he ha ha

Then, suddenly, this cheerful rag pile stands up to reveal a spirited old man. And what this old man says next is something that changes our lives **FOREVER**.

Not that. This...

The old man proceeds to describe a creature whose coat is that of **SOFT GOLDEN FLEECE.** A giant golden ram, if you will.

The fact that gold **EXISTS** in an almost thread-like form does sort of solve our time-crunch issue. But what the old man is telling us just seems way too convenient. Like it's **TOO** good to be true. However, you know what a good quester says about things that are too good to be true...sometimes they **ARE** true!

Moments later in the Dancing Pony tavern

As the pungent stranger puts down bowl after extra-beany bowl of the Dancing Pony's **FAMOUS CHILI**, he regales us with the remainder of his tale. Lesser questers might think that they were just being told what they wanted hear in exchange for free chili, but not me. I believe this man! Not so much for what he's told us, but more for what's about to happen next...

He is a **WIZARD!** Only a real-life wizard can disappear in a cloud of magic smoke. He was probably just lying in wait to impart **FANTASTIC KNOWLEDGE** upon a few worthy questers so that they might embark on a **FANTASTIC JOURNEY!** His story is 100 percent true because, as everyone already knows, magic=trustworthiness!

I know that the pile of rags Gil is pointing to is a **DIFFERENT** pile of rags. Sure, similar to the pile of rags from earlier, but in this case **NOT** housing a gassy wizard. Besides, who's to say that what the old man said wasn't true? Sometimes, all you need is just a little blind faith and a **CAN-DO ATTITUDE** to get you through the dark times of life!

The villager tells us that he doesn't care what we do, and that they're probably just going to make **STRAW VERSIONS** of themselves so the town doesn't look abandoned when the dragon comes back next year.

I tell the villager that their kindling doppel-gängers will not be needed. For the Quest Kids are now officially **ON THE QUEST!**

We leave at DAWN!

Rag pile farted again.

It was the **DOG!**

THPT

chili coma

CHAPTER 4

Before the start of any quest, it's important to gear up. Quests usually take some time, so making sure you have plenty of supplies to carry you through is key. My friends and I split up once again to visit the mountain village's **VARIOUS VENDORS**, and I stumble upon something I completely missed the first time around. A "Ye Ole Bagel Shoppe." We used to have one of those back home. Best bagels in Hamhaven! 'Til they closed, that is.

That voice? Can it be? I look behind the bagel counter and it's her. **JENNIFER!** This must be where she moved after her parents closed up shop in Hamhaven!

I would deliver freshly milled flour from our farm to Jennifer's bagelry back home. Man, I had the **BIGGEST CRUSH** on her. So did Gil. Whenever we'd pretend to quest as kids, Jennifer was the fair maiden Gil and I were saving.

I go by Ifer now.

Excuse me?

My name, it's Ifer. Short for Jennifer. I **NEVER LIKED** being called "Jen" all the time. So when we moved, I changed things up a bit.

I-fer.

No, **IFF**-er. Like there's two f's, but there really isn't, that's just **HOW** it's pronounced.

I watch her try to describe the **IMPOSSIBLY WEIRD** version of her name, and all of those old feelings come rushing ba-

So your family's moving here, too? I'd think twice. Bristolburg is often bothered by a **DEMANDING DRAGON**. Guess it wants a gold T-shirt now?

Actually, it's a gold track jacket. Yup, my friends and I are going to quest for one and, you know, probably **SAVE THE TOWN**. But whatever.

A **QUEST**? But you're a **FARMER**.

smolder face

Guess I sorta "changed things up a bit," too.

Your **PARENTS** let you quest?

My parents are gone.

Oh, I'm sorry.

Oh, it's okay, they're **NOT DEAD**.

Nope, they just **ABANDONED** me. That, or they were **ABDUCTED**. Which, when I say it aloud, isn't all that much better. But the point is, I started questing to **FIND** them. Haven't found them yet, though.

And well... I guess I haven't really been looking all that hard for them, either...

uncomfortable realization

ANYWAY, I heard about the whole dragon-pants thing and thought I'd lend muh **QUESTIN' SKILLS** here and what-not.

Oh, um, **GREAT.**

FLOUR

As I leave Ifer's bagel shop, I turn and watch her through the window. She smiles warmly at the next customer as she sniffs their bagels. And it's at this moment that the **TRUE WEIGHT** of our quest hits me. This wouldn't be just some random village we were attempting to save. This was Ifer's village, and it had a name. Bristolburg. And if we don't succeed, then every Bristolburgian waiting in line for warm bagels to bring home to their children, or their parents, or their grandparents, or even their pets...all of them will be made to suffer.

And we **CANNOT** let that happen.

CHAPTER 5

Fully stocked for our journey, we depart
Bristolburg early the next day. Our
group self-assuredly struts out of town,
knowing that we'd finally overcome the first
major hurdle of questing. **GETTING HIRED!**
And since we'll basically be questing for
a big yellow sheep, the rest, as they say,
should all be downhill.

Spellbound by my strut, I forget for a moment that Bristolburg is a mountain village. And mountain villages, by nature, tend to be located **IN THE MOUNTAINS.** And as you may or may not already know, mountains are tall and can have deadly ledges that will kill you, if you happen to walk off one of them. But, in my defense, there were some trees in the way.

Terra doesn't miss much. I only picked this way out of town because it's the opposite direction of the dragon's lair. But one should never let **MINOR THINGS** like having no idea which way to go stop one from questing. No quest would ever begin if all anyone did was ponder north, east, south, or west. So I always say just pick a direction and **BOOM**, you're questing!

Fine, guess we're gonna make a whole big to-do out of the almost-walking-my-questing-party-off-a-cliff-to-our-certain-deaths thing. No worries. A good quest leader can easily win favor again by simply **PROJECTING CONFIDENCE** and inspiring his questers with a few carefully chosen words.

It seems as though the seeds of doubt have already been sown, and no matter how **INCREDIBLY MOVING** my speech was, my friends are determined not to move until given good reason to. So when you can't persuade your questing party to blindly follow you without question, I find that it's a good idea to **CALL A MEETING.**

In a meeting, all members of your group should sit in a circle and face one another. This way you can discuss the issue at hand **OPENLY** and **FAIRLY.**

Yup, a meeting might just be the **SHOT IN THE ARM** your fledgling quest needs. But you mustn't forget the snacks. Meetings just seem to go way better if they're **CATERED.** Which is why I'm super glad I ran into Ifer yesterday!

KNOCK IT OFF!

We can't keep going in a direction we don't know is **RIGHT**, to find something we don't know is **REAL!**

sniff

Yeah, and I don't trust that raggedy wizard. He was **BONKERS!**

loopy

But if we do nothing, **IFER'S** village gets destroyed.

(cricket noises)

Who?

Oh, yes, they are! At least that's what Gazimar the Great taught me. There exists a great **CHRONICLED HISTORY** of all known events and creatures of this world. A library as old as time. Kept by creatures as old as time. **THE ELVES.**

elf.

Fine, the "Halls" are real. And they are kept by the Elves, but I **CAN'T** go back there.

They said if I ever returned, they would take my **OTHER EYE.**

AWESOME!!! I mean, not that Terra lost an eye. That must have hurt. But now we finally have some idea as to how she lost it. Sure, we all agree that Terra's eyepatch is **SUPER COOL**, but we're also **SUPER AFRAID** of getting punched if we ever bring it up. So we don't.

Knowing that she was **BANISHED** from her home makes her life that much more tragic. It now makes sense that she clings to our group of outcasts. She's an outcast herself.

Terra, I just don't **SEE** another way. No pun intended.

DON'T HURT ME!!

Ned's right. If there's a way to save Ifer, and, um, I guess all those other villagers, we should probably **TRY IT.**

There may be a way to make it into the "Halls" undetected, but it won't be easy. And if we're found, they may take **ALL** our eyes.

Terra's words send a shiver down my spine. I'm not a huge fan of pain and I generally try to avoid it, but Ifer's village is depending on us. **WE HAVE TO DO THIS**! Also, what is it with elves and eyes? It's a little weird, right?

Please, Terra, will you lead us to the **HALLS OF WISDOM**?

Terra pauses and takes a deep breath. She slowly lifts her head and somberly looks off into the distance. Then she points, and all at once our quest's **TRUE DIRECTION** is finally revealed.

Just saying, I **TOTALLY** was.

Concerning Dragons

a PONDERMENT *by* J.B. LÜCASTOOTHÉ

A dragon's love of gold is undeniable. Through many ancient texts, this has been a constant that holds true. However, their use of it remains a mystery. Dragons do not frequent the marketplace, so they do not need gold for **TRADE** or **PURCHASE**.

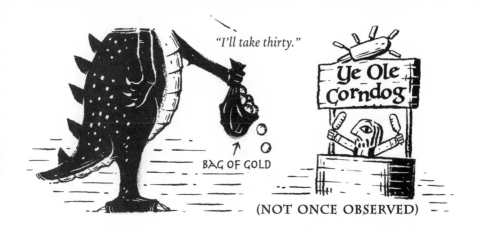

"I'll take thirty."

Ye Ole Corndog

BAG OF GOLD

(NOT ONCE OBSERVED)

When a dragon wants something like food or more gold,

it simply **TAKES** it.

"My shiny!"

YOINK

(OFTEN OBSERVED)

So then **WHY GOLD**? The nearest that can be

determined is that a dragon prefers to **SLUMBER** in,

on, or around it. But wouldn't a dragon choose to lounge

amongst straw or feather? Would this not make the

dragon much more comfortable? The dragon's mastery

of language points toward intelligence, so we can only

assume that it has tried this already.

Gold lounging is **NOT** a healthy practice. A dragon's desire to lie atop piles of gold has led to **SPINE MALFORMATIONS** over time.

(BEFORE GOLD LOUNGING)   (AFTER GOLD LOUNGING)

And the need to always be resting near their gold has only added to the beast's **OBESITY**.

DRAGON PAUNCH
↓

(AFTER MANY MANY YEARS OF GOLD LOUNGING)

This might just be the reason dragons are a rarity in the world today. They elect not to **VENTURE AWAY** from their precious gold for fear that it will be taken. And after years of inactivity, they end up lacking the ability to even move at all.

"Little help here?"

A situation only made **WORSE** by seasonal offerings.

But if ever given good reason to leave their gold-adorned lair, dragons are quite **FORMIDABLE**. And they will not soon forgive a slight against them until their perceived order of the world has been restored.

Ta-daaah!

CHAPTER 6

We've traveled two weeks through thick forest to find the Halls of Wisdom, only to be confronted by what appears to be just more **THICK FOREST.** Maybe Terra's confused. Actually, we're all feeling a little off, having subsisted mostly on seeds and berries ever since our road bagels mysteriously **VANISHED.**

One and a half weeks ago...

I don't understand. We should have, like, **FIFTEEN** left.

Perhaps in her weakened state, Terra has **FORGOTTEN** the way back to the land she was cast away from so very long ago.

Oh, I get it! We say the **MAGIC WORDS** and an entrance appears!

Here, let me try. "Meleuth, quitroo, gontureh!"*

*"My nose hair is lengthy!"

Gil reads Elvish a lot better than he speaks it, and his words lead to little in the way of door-opening. Terra tells us there's **NO MAGIC NEEDED.** In order to make it into the hidden realm of **ELVENDEMOR** undetected, we can simply use the "back way."

The tree's revelation sends a **BOLT OF EXCITEMENT** through our wearied group and we feel renewed once more. Descending the staircase takes us into the catacombs of Elvendemor, where the Elves bury their dead. Generations of elves are laid to rest here. It's a dark, cavernous place, as old as time itself.

It's wrong for us to be here. I get the uneasy
feeling that if we're discovered trespassing
in such a sacred space, it'll be a **PAINFULLY
PUNISHABLE** offense. Oh, well, we're here now
and as long as we leave everything exactly
as we found it, no one will be the wiser.

We ascend another staircase, which ends right below a **STONE CEILING.** Terra breaks the silence and whispers to us.

Directly above us resides **ALL** the knowledge the Elves possess after all our ages on this earth. Be **RESPECTFUL.** Non-elves have never laid eyes on it before.

..no.. ..more.. ..steps..

Why did she have to mention **EYES**?!

CHAPTER 7

'm not going to lie, I was expecting more. There seems to be **VERY LITTLE** in the way of "halls" and it looks like most of the "wisdom" has already been checked out for the day. The Elves must have been too pooped from digging burial tunnels to go on messing with their library.

How could this be all the knowledge of the known world since the beginning of time? Then Terra explains that this is **NOT EVERYTHING.** Before books, the Elves would inscribe their wisdom upon **SACRED SCROLLS.**

I see this as a **GOOD THING.** I'd been worried that we'd have thousands of books to comb through before finding anything about golden-fleeced rams. But if they do exist, it'll say so in one of these twenty-seven books or three scrolls.

HOLD UP!

I think I **FOUND** something!

Monsters, Creatures, and Other Junk and Stuff*

*Translated from Elvish

Gil reads from the ancient text, translating from Elvish as he goes. It feels like **ENCHANTED KNOWLEDGE** washing over us from across the ages. It's also riddled with grammatical errors.

It's like the Elves **DON'T KNOW** the difference between "their," "they're," and "there."

Yeah, and we're **NOT** great spellers, either.

Gil skips ahead.

"Beast of Gold"? Well, **THIS** looks promising.

"A **GOLDFISH**?"

YOLUAL.

There's only one entry. Apparently, there aren't too many beasts made of gold that have existed since the beginning of time. And assuming my non-elven knowledge isn't failing me, I'm pretty sure goldfish **AREN'T** actually made of gold.

We never should have listened to that old man. Rams with golden fleece? **RIDICULOUS.** It's clear to me now that we were lied to. Worse yet, Bristolburg is **DOOMED!**

Examining what's left of the ripped page, we can see a few wavy lines that could be hair, or fur, or, dare I say, **FLEECE**? And a couple of Elvish letters that Terra translates to a "G" and an "O." Maybe for **"GO-LDEN-FLEECED RAM"**?

WE HAVE THE PROOF WE NEED!

It's a couple letters and squiggly lines! We **DON'T KNOW** what it is!

Or maybe the page was ripped out because the creature is **EXTINCT.**

They wouldn't do that! These are the Halls of Wisdom, the legendary **ELVISH LIBRARY!**

the wisd

This library **STINKS.** No offense, Terra.

Yeah, it kinda does.

They're right, though. We aren't much better off than before. We have **NO CLUE** what was on that page or if it was even made of gold. It could be just another goldfish. Nope, it's obvious this is a dead end. To save the village, we need a **NEW PLAN.**

It's settled. We make the **DEAD GOLDFISH SWEATER.**

We need a plan other than that plan. But first we need to leave the Halls of Wisdom. I'm worried that we've already been here too long, and I don't want some elf gouging out my eyes just for seeing their **DUMPY LIBRARY.** We need to leave right now the same way we came in.

Or maybe we'll just stay just a bit longer.

CHAPTER 8

We're trapped. Well, sort of. We could have Boulder try to **SMASH** his way through. But it would be Boulder's stone hands against the stone floor. Meaning, either the floor breaks apart or Boulder's hands do, and Boulder likes having hands.

I guess we could just hang out in the library indefinitely. It doesn't seem like the Elves have too many reasons to visit. But staying put means **DOING NOTHING** to save Ifer's village, so we move toward the front door.

Don't worry. It's not even dawn yet. Everyone's **STILL** sleeping.

I won't lie, I'm **VERY NERVOUS** about the prospect of us being discovered. But part of me needs to see what's on the other side of that door. Few non-elves have ever witnessed the wondrous realm of Elvendemor. It's got to be **BETTER** than the library, right?

Well, he doesn't seem all that eye-poppingly angry. And he also knows Terra. It's almost like he's **HAPPY** to see her or something. The suspense is killing me, so I just ask...

Yeah, Terra, what **IS** going on? Why are our eyes not being boiled in some **FREAKY ELVEN** soup? Or being used for marbles, or ping-pong, or...okay, maybe I've built this up in my head too much, but it's clear that Terra has some explaining to do.

You know, cuz we elves are **WAY CRAZY** about eyes and **YOU ALL** took out one of mine before banishing me forever.

Um, you lost your eye in a **BIRDHOUSE BUILDING** accident.

WHAT?!

We go back into the library and Terra breaks
down for Darryl **EVERYTHING** that happened to
her since she left. Her meeting up with us, our
quest attempts, our recent encounter with the
dragon, and our current **WOULD-BE QUEST.**

Now this is all well and good for Darryl. I'm
glad he's getting the 411 on Terra's exploits,
but what about **US**? For the last two weeks
I've been completely terrified, and it turns
out the Elves are **WAY COOL** and aren't odd
in any way about eyes.

Terra was lying to us this whole time and
I don't like it.

Look, what Darryl said is true. I lost my eye in a **BIRDHOUSE BUILDING** accident.

How did you...

step

READ
the wisdom

When you live in a place where you have everything and time doesn't matter, you need a lot of hobbies to **PASS** the time. Mine was building birdhouses. I've probably built five thousand of them.

creak

No joke, we almost staged an intervention.

I had built so many that one day I was careless and **FORGOT** eye protection.

THUNK!

"The enchanted power-saw kicked a piece of wood in my eye."

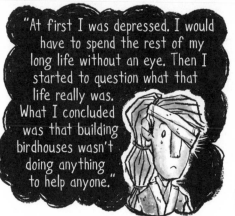

"At first I was depressed. I would have to spend the rest of my long life without an eye. Then I started to question what that life really was. What I concluded was that building birdhouses wasn't doing anything to help anyone."

You were helping birds.

Yes, but I wanted to do **MORE**.

"I spent the next 50 years honing my skills so I could make a difference."

mean eyepatch

outfitting

vacant birdhouse

kickboxing

arrow

marksmanning

vine-swinging

flaming mace   flaming axe

weapon-wielding

???

camouflaging

Oh, we all thought you were just going through a **PHASE**.

"Then I left home to strike out on my own."

Now Leaving Elvendemor

But it turns out I wasn't on my own. Because not only did losing my eye allow me to find **MYSELF**.

It also allowed me to find all of **YOU**.

I knew exactly what she meant. My mom and dad were **GONE.** And the simple truth was, if they had never disappeared, then I never would have met Terra, Boulder, or Ash.

As much as I miss my parents, and as much as I would give **ANYTHING** to have them back again, my life would just feel so empty without my friends.

CHAPTER 9

I t turns out the Halls of Wisdom hadn't always needed a guard. Darryl explains that there was a theft recently and they needed to **BEEF UP** security. This might explain why there were so few books. Perhaps the bandits made off with the **LION'S SHARE** of Elvish knowledge.

Nope, they just snagged **ONE SCROLL** and a half a roll of these **STICKERS**.

SCROLL BIN

scurry.

Well, I guess when you only have twenty-seven books and three scrolls, one missing scroll is quite a lot. Then Gil has the presence of mind to bring up the **MISSING PAGE** from the book we just read.

What about this **MISSING PAGE**? Did the bandits make off with that as well?

Darryl has been nothing but **JOVIAL** since
we met him, but the second Gil shows him the
book with the missing page, the color leaves
his face.

I get the impression that the reason was a
pretty good one. You don't go ripping out pages
from your slim collection of **ANCIENT TEXTS**
unless you absolutely have to. I'm just hoping
that at some point he decides to tell us why.

Terra's demand shakes Darryl from his **SPOOKY SILENCE.** And it seems Darryl was right to be weird and ominous, because what he shares with us next makes my face turn even paler than his.

Darryl walks to a **STORAGE CHEST** in the corner of the library. He shuffles through a ring of keys on his belt, finds the right one, and opens the lock on the chest. He brings over a single piece of paper, torn along the edges, and places it in front of us.

The beast on the page is not a golden-fleeced ram. It is something **SO TERRIBLE** that my eyes beg me to look away, but I can't. All I can picture is what this horrible creature must have done to the poor elf who found it.

Why anyone in their **RIGHT MIND** would go looking for that thing, I do not know. I mean, that elf must have been crazy or reckless or...

Or in love! Of course, the **CLASSIC TALE** of a brave knight attempting to save his fair maiden from the gruesome beast that took her. Then Darryl sits us down to tell us the **ILL-FATED** elf's real life story, which is altogether much more sorrowful.

"In a desperate search, he uncovered a page from an ancient text, describing a beast whose golden fleece was believed to extend or prolong life."

"The elf went out on his own to find this beast and save his beloved."

"But the elf never returned and his bride has long since passed on."

rip

"So the cursed page was removed to prevent other elves from meeting a similar fate."

We gotta find and shave that **RAGE BEAST!**

poof Poof

Did you not hear what I just said?

Ned's right. The beast's golden fleece is the **ONLY** way!

FOOLS! I understand that you two are in love. It was obvious from that super long hug earlier. But **HE** is mortal and you will all **DiE** if you go looking for this monster!

First off, gross! That was a **FRIEND HUG.**

Thanks for making it weird, man.

Don't worry, Darryl, we don't need the fleece to extend our lives.

Yeah, we're just using it to make a giant golden track jacket for a dragon.

Darryl doesn't seem **TOO CONVINCED**, but he still flips over the torn page to reveal a map on the back. Now it looks like our quest is **OFFICIALLY OFFICIAL.** We have something to find and an idea of how to find it. But instead of being super excited, I feel only dread. I look over at my friends and wonder if we will ever be coming back.

Yup, definitely time for a bathroom break.

CHAPTER·10

Darryl is not too keen on letting us take the torn page from their sacred book, so Terra **TRANSCRIBES** the map onto a piece of parchment. Which is fine by me, since the map is really all we need. And to tell you the truth, I don't want to stare at that terrifying picture of the **RAGE BEAST** for our entire quest. But Terra draws one of those, too.

I guess she devoted **MORE TIME** to perfecting birdhouses over the last 700 years than to art class. Who knows? Maybe her silly picture will make it **EASIER** for us to go on a quest that could very well end in our demise.

Needs **MORE BLOOD** around the fangs!

That's not important, **OKAY**?!

I flip Terra's page over and we compare our map against the original from the book to make sure **EVERY DETAIL** is correct.

Our road looks unfamiliar and **DANGEROUS.** It makes me wonder whether this poor elf even arrived at his destination or if he was felled along the way.

I try to make myself feel better, concentrating on the fact that this was just one elf who went on this quest. We have an elf, a wizard, a rock troll, and a pig-dog-thing. Our numbers alone should **INCREASE** our odds, right?

Are you sure you won't reconsider? The elf who first quested for this beast was our very best **WARRIOR PRINCE**. Thousands of years of experience. Never once a scratch in battle. He was quite literally the **BEST** of us.

toot!

Okay, so basically we're dead. I really feel like quitting now, but I can't. If I do, then Ifer's village gets destroyed. But here's the thing: It's not all up to me. If the best elf ever couldn't do it by himself, there's **NO WAY**

I'll be able to. If we're really going to go through with this as a team, then we need to **DECIDE** as a team.

This will be the most dangerous thing we've ever attempted. Before we set out on a quest that may be our **LAST**, I need to know if you're still with me.

step.

Terra steps forward. The bravest of us by far. Then Gil. Sweet, dependable Gil — my very best friend. Then Boulder, which fills me with great relief; I would not want to attempt such a quest without his strength. Then loyal Ash scuffles forward and snorts and smiles.

I could not ask for a better, **BRAVER** group of friends.

I didn't think I was in the bathroom for that
long. I won't lie. I am a little disappointed, but
I get it. This won't be as easy as questing
for **GOLD SHEEP.** I know that they're afraid,
and that it's just the **FEAR TALKING.** They
don't want to die, and I don't, either. Then
I remind them why we got into this quest in
the first place. For Ifer and the rest of the
villagers. For Bristolburg.

Ifer could move again?

Yeah, and it wouldn't be the first village we left in ruins. Anyone remember **QUEST ATTEMPT 2**?

bars

YES! QUIT REMINDING ME!!

And if the **BEST ELF EVER** never came back, what chance do **WE** have?

WE have each other.

What if **WE** end up dead? What good are we to the village then?

I think this strikes a chord with the group.
But then Gil offers up **ONE MORE** point.

Gil's right, we're young and inexperienced
and don't know anything about the world.
And part of this inexperience led to one
village being **BURNED TO THE GROUND.**
We can't do anything about that now, but
we **CAN** do something about this.

I **KNOW** we can do this.

Ned, it's nice that you believe in us, but this is the **REAL** world.

No, you don't understand, I know we can do this because...um, a **MYSTIC** told me.

A mystic? What mystic?

After my parents disappeared, I sought out a mystic for answers. She told me I would quest for my parents with a **BRAVE** group of friends.

A boy **WIZARD**, a friend made of **STONE**, an **ELF** with one eye, and some kind of **PIG** that was also maybe a **DOG** but probably also **SOMETHING ELSE** mixed in, too.

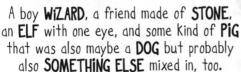

She said we would **TRIUMPH** over a beast of gold. I thought for sure she meant that dragon. That's why I was so confident we could depants it. But now I know she was referring to an **ACTUAL** beast of gold.

My friends, together we can save Bristolburg. It has been **FORETOLD.** Let's accept our destiny and **DO THIS.**

Hold up, are you **CAT-DANGLING** again?

Cat-dangling?

You know, telling us what we want to hear so we'll go on this quest?

Cat? Me? I don't—

Ned would never use his missing parents in some sort of **HALF-BAKED** lie!

Um...yeah?

I guess if you really wanted to cat-dangle, you could've just mentioned any number of the **FERAL CATS** roaming Bristolburg that we'd be saving. Which, when I say it aloud, is reason enough for me. I'm in. Look at that—cat-dangled myself.

I'm in, too! But first, did the mystic foresee me having **A CHANCE** with Ifer?

woosh

You're probably not running into any other **ONE-EYED ELVES** along the way, so I guess I'm going, too.

tug tug snort

With arms outstretched, we gather close together and tightly hold hands. A questing party, **UNITED**, with a clear goal in mind. Whether or not the final outcome was actually foreseen or not isn't important. We're together now, and that's what we'll need if we'll have any chance at...

HELLO?! Sorry to break up the FEEL-GOOD FEST, but did your "mystic" happen to mention how you'll go about SHAVING an insane bloodthirsty rage beast?!

Just saying, cuz that morsel of info might prove a wee bit useful.

(clueless silence)

Darryl's right. This is no longer some docile sheep sitting idly by, waiting to be sheared. It'll be the **DEADLIEST THING** we've ever faced. The truth is, I have no plan. Just an unwavering belief in my friends. Maybe I'm naive, but I really do feel **DESTINED** to have found them. And somehow I know, if we all stick together, we're going to figure everything out. I don't need a mystic to tell me this, even if that's exactly what my friends need to hear right now.

She said it would all be clear when the time comes, and in the end, **WE** would triumph.

So it has been **FORETOLD.**

Mapping a Quest

a BREAKDOWN OF PERILS *by* J.B. LÜCASTOOTHÉ

n estled amongst the pages of the field guide I excavated so many years ago is a map transcribed by the elf ranger, Terra. This section will serve as an **OVERVIEW** of this map, outlining the perils to be faced by the Quest Kids on their journey to find and shave a giant golden rage beast.

All good quests should have maps. For those unfamiliar with them, maps are what people used in the Middle Ages to find their way around **BEFORE** they owned cell phones.

As you can see, Terra has included **ALL** of the major hallmarks of a good map: a compass rose, a path, and a clear labeling of deadly perils.

PERIL 1: THE ACID SWAMPS OF DOOM

As near as can be determined, the Acid Swamps of Doom are just that. Swamps filled with deadly acid. Few venture into such a putrid place. I wonder if it's the name. Just a thought, but maybe the Acid **SPRINGS** of Doom would attract more people. Anyway, assuming the Quest Kids aren't completely burned alive by acid, they face a second peril which is, well, pretty annoying.

PERIL 2: THE INVISIBLE FOREST OF MADNESS

Some people have trouble seeing the forest for the trees, but with this forest that is literally the issue. No one makes it through without bumping their heads, like, **A LOT**. That or they just lose their minds. For it is a maze where one cannot see the walls. Acid baths and cranial contusions aside, the Quest Kids face one more impossible peril before reaching their final goal.

PERIL 3: VAGUELANDIA

Not much is known about Vaguelandia. But it's the third peril, so we can all assume that it's **PROBABLY** not great. I mean, you'd think it would be worse than the first two, right? I don't know, maybe it's okay, I guess.

If the Quest Kids are somehow still around after facing these perils, then they must confront the most dangerous peril of all.

FINAL PERIL: GOLDEN-FLEECED RAGE BEAST

Wow, that thing looks **MEAN**. Like rip-your-face-off mean. Maybe consider not reading any more of this book if you like remembering the Quest Kids with faces. It's enough to make you lose your appetite.

Ooh! Which reminds me of the last thing that all good maps need. **REST STOPS**!

REST STOP: BIG FRIAR'S FRYER

Big Friar's Fryer is a delightful little brunch dive tucked away on the road to the Acid Swamps. The perfect eatery for would-be questers looking to **CARB UP** before marching toward impending doom.

CHAPTER 11

As we travel down this new road, guilt begins creeping in. Not the **GASTRIC** guilt I'm sure to be feeling five miles from now. It's the guilt for once again lying to my friends and knowing that this time it may cost us. Gil senses that I'm a little off and checks in.

She's old enough to be your **GRANDMA**, you know.

Gil and I *go* way back. He knows me better than anyone else in the world. When I'm down, he always says the **PERFECT THING** to cheer me up. Except, that is, for right now.

Well, she'd actually be your grandma's grandma's grandma's **GRANDMA.**

I continue to look at him quizzically, but then clue in that he's talking about Terra. She's 700 years old, which in terms of grandmas is not all that far off. I still don't know what this has to do with anything, so my expression doesn't change.

The way you two were hugging. The **AGE DIFFERENCE** makes it weird.

Gil thinks I have a thing for Terra. It was a **FRIEND HUG**! Besides, calling her "grandma" a million times is really killing it for me. In the interest of clearing the air about the "hug" and to also stop him from saying "grandma" again, I explain myself.

It's not like that. I just sort of understand Terra for the very **FIRST TIME.**

Is it because you both **LIED**?

I never lied! The mystic is real! **REAL**, I tell ya!

Um, no? She lied to us about her missing eye, like, that **ONE** time and you've cat-dangled everybody, like, a **HALF A DOZEN** times.

Oh, right. I do feel kinda bad for getting so mad at her about lying.

Guess I don't really have the best track record.

Just a **WEE BIT** hypocritical.

So then what was it?

What was what?

It feels both good and bad to finally get that off my chest. I know Gil won't judge me. But it's still a **HORRIBLE THING** to think, let alone say out loud.

My parents always said there's nothing more noble in life than growing food for others.

But that life just wasn't for me. I wanted a **QUESTER'S LIFE**, like my aunt and uncle had. My parents would proudly regale me with tales of my aunt and uncle's adventures over many a dinner. **EPIC STORIES** almost too fantastic to be true, but always told with a hint of sadness and longing. For my aunt and uncle perished before I was born.

Whenever I brought up my own dreams of questing, that same look of despair would well up in their eyes. They didn't want me to meet a similar fate. I understood, but I also felt **TRAPPED.** And then there came a day when I just couldn't deny who I was any longer.

I ran away.

What?

I made it as far as the natural spring just outside our village. I stopped and stared at the full moon reflecting in the spring's midnight-blackened pools. I remembered hiking to the spring with my parents when I was young. Whenever we passed by, they'd always tell me to make a wish. I made a **NEW WISH** that night.

I just wished to not be a farmer anymore. And if that meant I had to **RUN AWAY**, so be it. But the thought of my parents waking up and finding me missing...I just couldn't put them through that. So I hid in the caves near the spring until dawn and then went home.

"But when I got back, they were already gone."

They must have ventured out looking for me. It's **MY FAULT** that they're gone, Gil.

Ned, if that's true, then why'd Gazimar disappear the very **SAME NIGHT?**

Gil has a point. The timing of his teacher's disappearance does seem way too **COINCIDENTAL.** And if my parents had gone out looking for me, then why didn't they just check back in to see if I'd come home? Still, I can't help but feel that if I hadn't run away that night, then maybe, just maybe, they'd still be here.

What'd the mystic say?

Pardon?

The **MYSTIC**—the one you went to see about your missing parents?

Oh, right, um, she said that it was just all **TOO HAZY** to see.

Then I'll tell you what **I SEE**.

grab

I see us finding your parents, Ned. And **WHEN** we do, they'll hug you and tell you how much they **LOVE YOU**. Then you'll see that all of this had **NOTHING** to do with you. I promise.

Okay, maybe I'm not the reason my parents are missing. But I do know that I haven't just been lying to my friends; I've been lying to myself. I've been distracting us with all of these other quests for a reason. Because I'm **NOT READY** to find my parents. Deep down, I know that when I do, this life, my questing life, will be over.

CHAPTER 12

A big meal before a quest is essential. You never know when you'll find food again, so you should **PACK UP** as much of it as possible. As we fill our bellies and our pockets full of the Friar's Fryer's finest pancakes, I study our map. Upon leaving the safety of our breakfast oasis, we'll head directly to the first obstacle, the Acid Swamps of Doom.

They probably could have left off the "of Doom" part. The "Acid Swamps" by itself is pretty **OFF-PUTTING.** Unless they're trying to differentiate these acid swamps from other acid swamps that are only somewhat acidic. Like this delicious orange juice.

I don't know what to tell Terra. According to the map, the swamp looks fairly wide. There's no way we're crossing it by jumping or with an impressively long **POLE VAULT**. Plus, I've never pole vaulted and I wouldn't want my first attempt to be over a bog of **BODY-DISSOLVING ACID.**

The helpful waiter points in the direction of a dark figure sitting in the corner of the room. The mere sight of him chills me to my very core. The figure has the look of **DEATH** itself and does not give off much of a "Larry" vibe.

B-behind the **SCYTHE GUY**?

Good ol' Larry, looking terrifying as always. Boat rides only cost **ONE** silver piece each!

Well, the waitstaff here seems to think pretty highly of Larry. And he's **REALLY** putting away those pancakes, so how bad can he be?

One silver piece? That's a **BARGAIN**! What do you guys think?

Larry **STINKS**. Let's not talk about him.

Larry will devour our **SOULS** like a stack of hotcakes.

The thing about appearances is that they can be deceiving. Sure, someone can look a little rough on the outside, but maybe deep down they're **GOOD PEOPLE.** You just need to get to know them a little better.

I slowly make my way across the room and over to Larry. As I get closer, the **ROOM DARKENS** and becomes colder. I find it harder and harder to breathe, as if someone or something is pushing down on my chest. The only sound I can hear is my own racing heartbeat. Then I arrive at Larry's **COZY BREAKFAST NOOK.**

My friends and I are interested in passage to the other side.

flip

Cruises times are daily at 10, 12, 2, and 4. CRAZY LARRY'S ACID SWAMPS OF DOOM ADVENTURE CRUISES LLC. is not responsible for any lost or broken items, or unexpected maimings, mutilations, and certain deaths.

COOL! Can I keep this? I just wanna show it to my friends.

The restaurant warms again as I cross the room back to our table. Once more, I hear the sounds and voices of the other guests. My friends seem **FROZEN IN TIME**, appearing not to have moved since I left them.

CHAPTER 13

As swamps go, this one looks pretty normal. Well, except for all of the bubbling, and the acrid sulfury smell, and the lack of any wildlife at all. I start to wonder how it is we are going to make it across. What manner of watercraft can withstand such **HARSH CONDITIONS**?

I'm **SUPER IMPRESSED.** Aside from it being entirely made of bones, it's really a fine boat. Expert craftsmanship all the way! Larry holds out his hand for payment. I show him five silver pieces, but tell him that we'd prefer to settle up once we've made it across safely. Larry seems to have no problem with that and waves us aboard.

Larry hands me a waiver to sign, along with a request form for our desired cruise.

As much as I would like to learn more about The Acid Swamps of Doom wildlife, and we could actually use the team building, I simply choose passage to the other side. Larry pushes away from the dock with an oar that I can only assume is also **MADE OF BONE.**

Larry navigates us through the swamp, careful
not to splash the acid into the boat or onto us,
for that matter. I admit, it's tough giving up
control to someone you don't know that well. And
being surrounded by pools of skin-eroding acid,
our group couldn't feel more **VULNERABLE.** Some
of us are dealing with this better than others.

I quietly explain that passage to the other
side must be just **UNDER AN HOUR,** since
Larry's cruise times throughout the day are
spaced about two hours apart. One hour there
and one hour for Larry to get back. This seems
to relax everyone.

I wonder what makes something a swamp as opposed to another body of water. This could be an Acid **POND** of Doom or an Acid **LAKE** of Doom for all we know. There's no vegetation or animals to distinguish it from anything else.

What would Larry have even talked about on his wildlife tour? He seems to be a man of few words anyway, so maybe that all works out. But I just can't help myself, so I ask.

So, Larry, why do they call this a **SWAMP** anyway? Looks more like a **LAKE** to me.

Larry again says nothing, and then just points to one side of his bony craft. At first, I don't see anything. Then, I **LOOK CLOSER** and notice some small round whitish shapes floating in the acid.

Acid splashes onto the boat, **NARROWLY MISSING** us, but landing on Boulder's life vest. He panics as we try to remove it before the acid eats its way through. Somehow, we unlatch the vest in time and Boulder **CHUCKS IT** into the swamp.

Apparently, they went with the Acid **SWAMPS** of Doom because not only are we surrounded by **FLESH-EATING** acid, but that acid is teeming with **FLESH-EATING** bone-gators. A tad too much **FLESH-EATING** for my taste.

Sorry, Larry. Um, we'll **PAY YOU BACK** for the vest.

Not that there's any point to wearing a life vest out here. They seem to **BURN** just as easily as we would, and probably would only keep us afloat long enough to be gorged down by a bone-gator.

I move to the center of the boat and really start to worry. I don't see how our present situation can get any more dangerous. Then I think, as terrifying as bone-gators are to us, Larry doesn't seem too worried. It's just **SIMPLE WILDLIFE** that he deals with every day.

It feels like we've been out here for about a half-hour, so we should nearly be halfway across. We're almost done. The Quest Kids can endure the Acid Swamps just a bit longer. **WE GOT THIS!**

Then again, maybe this is something we don't got.

Here, boy! Time to get off the **TERRIFYING** bone-gator now.

CHAPTER 14

sh is a good pig-dog-thing. It would pain me very much to see him go. But sometimes you just can't save someone from themselves. And if that someone wants to get their kicks **RIDING ATOP** a deadly bone-gator, floating in a pool of acid, who am I to stop them? But the thing is, Ash doesn't know any better. Yes, he's a weird pig-dog-thing who chokes at every meal and would have died over a thousand times if we weren't around; but he's also **OUR** weird pig-dog-thing, and we love him.

Being the one made of rock, Boulder reaches out to Ash. He has the best chance of not having his arms **RIPPED OFF.** That whole being MMOR thing is usually how Boulder is elected to do whatever it is we don't want to.

Ash is totally oblivious to the certain death surrounding him and just stares at Boulder. I can tell Boulder is getting nervous. He's starting to **SWEAT.** You wouldn't think a rock could perspire, but Boulder does. **BIG TIME.**

We stare helplessly into the swamp and see nothing. The acid must have been so powerful that it **MELTED HIM** as soon as he fell in. Ash didn't stand a chance!

Everyone turns their gaze in my direction.
Nobody comes out and says it, but I can see
that they **BLAME ME.** And they're not wrong.
When you're the leader, anything good or bad
that happens on your quest is ultimately your
responsibility.

Tears stream down my face and into the acid. What have I done? Facing our first real peril on our first real quest and we've already **LOST SOMEONE.** Maybe I'm not cut out to lead. Maybe we should just turn back.

Then I notice that the raft has stopped. I look at Larry who usually looks like Death, but now he looks as though he's seen Death, only not the kind that looks like him. Nope, this is something that he's **NEVER EVER** laid eyes on before.

shakka shakka

CHAPTER 15

When we started the day, none of us had ever seen a real-life alligator before, certainly never one **MADE OF BONES.** And we'd

RISE

certainly never seen a bone-gator **THIS BIG.**
The concerning thing is that this seems to be a
brand-new experience for our boat captain, too.

Larry starts paddling backward, but at a rate that isn't all that much faster than before. Definitely **NOT** at the pace needed to elude a bone-gator of this size.

I close my eyes and wait for the creature to strike, knowing that when it does, we'll either be **SNAPPED** in half or **DISSOLVED** by acid. I can't decide which would be worse. Oh well, at least we'll be with Ash soon, wherever that is. Then the boat rocks violently, and I open my eyes.

ROCK BEATS GIANT BONE-GATOR! Way to go, Boulder. Boulder shakes as he holds the monster at bay, keeping it from breaking us to pieces. The boat rocks side to side, splashing acid all over, which Terra, Gil, and I try to dodge.

I would like to help Boulder, but all I can manage to do is **SHRIEK LIKE A TODDLER** every time acid splashes near me. I frantically search for something that could save us. Then I spot it. The oar! I pry it away from Larry's death grip and jam it into the beast's open jaw.

Momentarily stunned with its mouth lodged open, the giant bone-gator **DOESN'T KNOW** what to think. I shoot a look back at Larry, signaling to him that it's time to go. But Larry only shrugs and blankly stares back at me.

Our victory is **SHORT-LIVED** as the giant bone-gator snaps Larry's oar in two. Then it rears its head back, readying itself for the final strike. We appear to be dead in the water, or rather, dead in the bone-gator–infested body-dissolving acid. Which, now as I say it, makes perfect sense. Anyway, we all brace for impact.

Then a **SUDDEN JOLT** from behind knocks us over and launches us forward.

We **JET PAST** the giant bone-gator as if we were being pushed forward by a team of our very own bone-gators. But I look back and see that this isn't the case at all.

It's just one very flatulent pig-dog-thing.

I've never been so happy to see the gassy little guy. Not only am I ecstatic he's not an acidified **PUDDLE OF GOO**, but he's also saving our lives!

I guess the "thing" portion of our pig-dog-thing is most likely **DRAGON**, and his scaly skin is protecting him from the acid. The barrage currently blasting from his **BACKSIDE** must be due to all of the acid he swallowed on his way to the bottom of the swamp. Normally, when Ash throws wind, he has a look of contentment, but let's just say that right now he appears **UNCOMFORTABLE.**

We **CLOSE IN** on the other side of the swamp and as happy as I am that we're no longer near the jaws of a giant bone-gator, I am equally concerned that we're going to hit shore like we're being dropped from the sky. Fortunately, I don't have too much time to think about this.

I black out the second we make contact. I don't know how long I was unconscious, maybe a couple minutes? I slowly get up and look around for my friends, who are hopefully still alive amongst the **SCATTERED WRECKAGE** of Larry's boat.

Thankfully, everyone seems fine. Which we all owe to Ash. We track down the little guy and once again he has that look of **CONTENTMENT**. The worst of it being behind him.

There's no trace of Larry, though. Just pieces of **BROKEN BONES** from his boat. But for all we know, any one of those bones could be his. Either that or he fell into the acid swamp.

I feel bad. I know it wasn't exactly our fault. We didn't mean for Larry to lose his boat, and probably his life. But if Ash hadn't saved us from that giant bone-gator the way he did, there's a good chance that we'd **ALL** be dead.

He was scary, but okay, I guess.

He was a man of few words.

makeshift grave

He liked pancakes.

And being creepy.

We do our best to **HONOR** Larry's memory. We knew him only briefly, but we all feel his loss. Still, I can't help but be thankful that we're not holding a memorial for Ash right now. And then I look around at my friends and I wonder if our quest's **FINAL TOLL** won't end up costing us much, much more.

silver pieces

Questing and Loss

a SUPPLEMENT *by* J.B. LÜCASTOOTHÉ

To gain is the goal for every able quester, whether in the form of a **LIFE SAVED** or the procurement of a **LOST TREASURE**. But, all too often, quests can bring about loss. To put it in **TODAY'S TERMS** that everyone understands, it's like when one of your ferrets misses their morning roll call. And you're like, hello, there were twenty-five ferrets yesterday, why are there only twenty-four today? And then you start **QUESTIONING YOURSELF** and are, like, did I really have twenty-five ferrets? Then you totally list the names of all twenty-five ferrets, and you're like, yeah, I really did have twenty-five ferrets. Anyway, that's probably how Ned feels right about now. Proof of which can be found in a letter I found folded inside the back cover of his manuscript.

Dearest Mom and Dad,

If you're reading this, then I didn't make it out
of this quest alive. Hopefully, my friends survived
and somehow found you or you happened upon them.
But as much as I hate to think about it, it's a **REAL
POSSIBILITY** that none of us made it out. So whether
this letter reaches you or not, I just needed to say
a few things.

I'm sorry for not being stronger. I wish I'd had the
courage to talk to you about who I really was. But
after you lost your family to questing, I thought
it better to **KEEP THAT TO MYSELF.**

We've taken on this latest quest to help a village
full of people. Hopefully, you'd be **PROUD** of that.
But I can't help feeling that I'm only doing it so
I won't have to confront you. I don't know, maybe
I'm overthinking it. Even if we abandoned this quest
today, I wouldn't have the faintest clue how to
find you.

- OVER -

I still have a hard time wrapping my mind around your disappearance. If you were taken from me, why was there **NO SIGN** of struggle? If you went out looking for me, then why didn't you **COME BACK**? And if you just abandoned me...well, I think that bothers me the most. That you left me of your own free will, and now you both have somehow made your peace with it.

I know I may not have been perfect, but I still loved you both with **EVERYTHING** I had. And if I ever do make it out of this quest alive, I promise that **I WILL FIND YOU**, whether you still want to be found or not.

Forever your son,

Ned

CHAPTER 16

We buried Larry three days ago and now we are **LOST.** There's no guide for this leg of our journey and according to our map we should have arrived at the Invisible Forest of Madness by now. But of course, it's invisible, so maybe we **MISSED IT.**

It looks to be just barren landscape, but we soon realize that this transparent forest is thick and **OVERGROWN.** We can't move an inch without hitting a branch, tripping over a root, or getting scratched by a thorn.

Moving in a specific direction is difficult, as the forest seems to have its **OWN OPINION** about where we should go.

As the sun sets, I realize that we should have slept before entering the forest. But that might be part of its allure, allowing you to almost see the other side, letting you think it's less dangerous than it really is. Once inside, you soon discover **OTHERWISE.**

We eventually find what we think is a clearing and set up camp.

We don't dare attempt moving at night. Not
that it affects our view of the forest, but
we can't risk getting separated and losing
sight of each other. We also forgo a fire.
Should the Invisible Forest catch flame, we'd
be **ENGULFED IN FLAMES** as well.

I close my eyes and my thoughts drift
toward my parents. I try to picture them
alive and safe. But then I start feeling bad
again for not looking for them. I'm a terrible
son. Going on other quests while they're still
out there? What am I trying to prove? My
guilt overtakes me and I **SPIRAL DOWNWARD.**

Mom? Dad? Is that you?!

I'm starting to see why they included the "of Madness" part in the forest's name. It was not by any means a restful night's sleep, and in the light of morning we can see that we're still closer to the entrance than to the other side. But going back is **NOT AN OPTION.** Not that the forest would even let us.

The daylight also reveals **SOMETHING ELSE.**
What might have been mistaken for a rock
the night before becomes all too apparent.
This rock shines like old armor. And it has two
legs. It's the body of a fallen knight.

Or perhaps a lovelorn prince.

CHAPTER 17

After spending the morning contorting through assorted varieties of invisible brush, we finally make it to the **ARMORED RELIC.** It's almost like the poor knight leaned up against a tree and just gave up. No great battle with a dragon or golden beast. Simply bested by an enemy he was surrounded by but couldn't see.

If it is him, I can't help but think of the one he left behind. A wife who never really knew what happened to him. How she must've hoped in vain for his return, and how she probably felt responsible that he never had. I shake my head. This could be **ANYONE.**

As always, Gil makes a lot of sense, and I get that sinking feeling once more. It's easier to **SEE** an enemy, no matter how horrible it is. At least you could move out of its way. With this forest, you're just stuck. Luckily, there's no way for us to know for sure who this was.

That's definitely **ELVISH** armor.

Seriously, Terra?!

I'm sure it's not **THE** elf Darryl spoke of. There are **A LOT** of elves out there.

I suppose a heavily armed sheep herder is also out of the question. Fine, it's everyone's favorite **LOVELORN ELF PRINCE**, conveniently equipped for rage beast de-fleecing. Only he never made it that far. Why? Was he too lorn with love and distracted to be thinking straight? Was he maybe just bad with directions? Or is this **HOPELESS PLACE** going to do to us what it did to him?

Terra waves the ancient shears past my face. I'm not sure what manner of Elvish craft went into their creation, but somehow after all these centuries, they still look like they were **FORGED YESTERDAY.** And yet, stuck out here year after year, lying in wait, never having fulfilled their purpose, we now happen upon them. The **PERFECT TOOL** we'll need to complete our quest. Does this mean something?

As much as I want this revelation to carry us forward, Terra is right. There's still no clear plan for how we'll be able to use these shears on the rage beast. Just the cryptic encouragement of a "mystic" saying everything's gonna be just fine. I don't know if my friends believe that anymore, and I don't bring it up again, either. Because, right now, stranded out here, standing over the bones of the world's most accomplished elf, our **ULTIMATE DESTINY** feels closer to his.

Remember when we were **BIRD BABIES?**

Boulder has a knack for zoning out when things get too stressful. He sits down, finds his happy place, and becomes an immovable, well, rock. It is both annoying and endearing. As I look over at my passive friend, I realize again what makes the Quest Kids different than the previous owner of these shears. That elf was alone. We **ARE NOT.** The biggest thing I've learned in my eleven years is that I don't know everything. That I **NEED** other people. I quest with friends because whenever I can't think of something to save us, someone else does.

Yeah, Quest Attempt 3. We were abducted by a **GIANT BiRD.** How is this relevant?

I was just looking up at the birds in that invisible tree and remembered how **SAFE** I felt in that giant bird's nest. You know, once it was clear it wasn't gonna eat us.

I hadn't felt that safe since before my parents left me.

We don't ever talk about what Boulder went through. About being **LEFT FOR DEAD**, once it was clear to his rock troll parents that he'd rather play with the other kids than bash their faces in.

That's nice, Boulder. I'm glad you felt that way.

Boulder's nice **LITTLE DETOUR** quiets our group for a moment and we begin to collect ourselves. No decision made in a state of panic is a wise decision. If you lose your head, especially in a place like this, then you're already done for. Like this poor ancient elf.

Maybe this is how the "madness" starts. After all hopelessness sets in, someone brings up something about birds and then everyone dies thinking a **HUGE SPARROW** is going to swoop down and save them.

They've all **LOST IT!**

Everyone just creepily stares and smiles at me as I cradle the trail mix, like they all know something that I don't. Either that or they're just planning to poke me full of feathers and ride me out of here as their **SAVIOR CHICKEN.**

CHAPTER 18

I sometimes forget that Gil is a wizard. I know the pointy hat and the long white beard are a dead giveaway, but he seldom uses magic. Mostly because he hasn't mastered very much of it. Sure, he was Gazimar the Great's star pupil, but he was also his **ONLY** pupil. And I don't think they dove into all that

much spell-casting before Gazimar vanished.
I rarely request magic from Gil because he
either gets defensive about not knowing very
much, or he casts a spell in not quite the
right way and things go **TERRIBLY WRONG.**

There's actually a spell for **THIS?**

I'm glad I'm not a wizard. No offense to the
practice of wizarding, but it's **BIZARRE.** Aside
from the crazy outfits, what is it with these
insanely specific spells? Did a wizard one day
say, "Hey, you know what I need right now?
A bird. And not just any bird. A really really
big one. I know, let's summon it!"

This is what makes me nervous. Knowing most of anything is not knowing **ALL** of it. What if you say the wrong thing and end up summoning a giant bloodthirsty badger?

Oh well, the rest of the group seems pretty excited about this for some reason. And the fact that Gil wants to try some magic is probably good for his magic shyness. Honestly, being mauled by a giant badger, as horrific as it sounds, would be **QUICKER** than losing all sense of direction, going mad, and starving to death. So let's **DO THIS!**

According to the spell preparations, we'll need a **FIRE.**

BOOK 'O' SPELLS

step

Great, the one thing we couldn't make last night to keep warm, because we'd risk being enveloped in **INVISIBLE WOODED FLAME,** is the one thing we'll need to cast this ridiculous spell.

Fine, being **BURNED ALIVE**, as horrific as it sounds, would also probably be a quicker death; so I guess we're still doing this. But we need to take as many precautions as possible.

So that's what we do the rest of the day. We feel our way around to find the most open clearing possible. Then we **MOVE EVERY** transparent log, thicket, and blade of grass we touch. I'm not going to lie. It's not super fun.

I know you can't tell from the drawing because everything is invisible, but you'll just have to trust me. It was **A LOT** of work.

(4 hours later)

My wizard robe is a **SWEATY SPONGE.**

We spend the next half hour **RECOVERING** from the afternoon's chore. Everyone fills up on the last of our trail mix. We arrange a few stones in a circle and collect some invisible kindling for a small fire. It is dusk now. Time for the ceremony to begin.

CHAPTER 19

We stare up at the sky for half the night. Watching. Waiting. But as beautiful as the stars are, one by one we fall asleep. Each of us experiences the kind of deep restful slumber that only arrives after being worked to **EXHAUSTION,** our dreams now filled with the possibility of what tomorrow might bring.

First off, **RUDE!** Can't I just visit without you thinking I'm going to charbroil you? I'm not a **MONSTER**, for Pete's sake!

Um...sorry???

It's fine. I guess I did try to **INCINERATE** you the last time we met. But it still **HURTS**, you know?

Oookay, then to what do we owe the pleasure?

Don't know, just felt the urge to fly out and check on you guys.

Wait, what? You felt an **URGE**?

Yeah, it was all drafty, and I was like, "I wish I had my track jacket right now. Wonder how the Quest Kids are doing."

woosh (shiver)

MY SPELL WORKED!!!

What spell?

Nothing! My friend is just **QUEST WEARY** and not thinking straight.

Pull

Oh, yes, I am! I did a **SUMMONING** spell last night and now you're here!

I don't feel summoned. I was just a little **CHILLY**, like I said.

Really? Then how'd you just happen to find us in the middle of the night?

I just felt an **URGE** to go this direction.

A **STRONG** urge?

Pretty strong as urges go, I guess.

I totally summoned you. My magic **WORKED!**

Fine, I was summoned! Dude, your friend's kind of a **DORK.**

Sorry, he just doesn't get to use his magic much.

YES! YES!

Enough!

Yeah, quit interrupting the **SMART ONE**.

We need **HELP**. We're stuck in this invisible forest and can't get out.

Is that what this is? I'm getting poked in, like, **EVERY** direction.

Yeah, those are invisible trees.

I didn't think that was a thing.

Kinda cool, but also **HORRIBLE**.

What about thorn bushes? Are those invisible, too?

Yeah, I got poked with one while we were clearing brush yesterday. I was, like, **WHAT** is that?

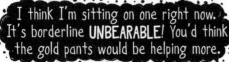

I think I'm sitting on one right now. It's borderline **UNBEARABLE!** You'd think the gold pants would be helping more.

Anyhoo, **CIRCLING BACK** to what Terra was saying. We could kinda use your help getting out of here.

Mmm, don't know about that. Helping with quests isn't really muh **THANG.**

It would get us one step closer to finding you your **GOLDEN TRACK JACKET.**

I **DO** really want that jacket...

Then you'll **HELP US?**

Well, I am your **FRIEND,** aren't I?

FRIEND? I thought we were doing this so the crazy dragon wouldn't burn down the village?

I think that's **VAGUELANDIA** down there. Or not. The map's kinda unclear.

Wait, have I been there before?

CHAPTER 20

There's a common misconception that you have to complete every part of a quest. Each obstacle builds upon the last, making you that much better prepared for when you face the final challenge. That's all well and good if those obstacles don't end up obliterating you first. And whoever came up with that rule certainly didn't have access to their very own **FLYING DRAGON.**

Um, hey. I, uh, just wanted to apologize.

What for?

When we found the elf prince back there, you know, the **DEAD** one?

I'm familiar.

Well, things looked pretty bleak, and I started to **DOUBT** what you said about the mystic.

Terra, don't...

Let me finish. Cuz now things feels **LESS** bleak. And with the dragon helping us, maybe shaving an insane rage beast isn't so...**INSANE**.

Sorry for doubting you. Just know that I will never **EVER** do that again. Because friendships are built on trust.

Yeah...trust...

And I **TRUST** you.

hug

205

I turn to Terra and open my mouth so that something **TRUTHFUL** has the chance to spill out of it. Something that could actually earn her trust for real. But nothing comes out. I can't tell her the truth right now. I just can't.

Because, mystic or not, our mission has momentum now, and I'm not going to mess with that. If we play our cards right, maybe we can persuade the dragon to sit on the rage beast while we clipper it or something. I dunno, I don't have it sorted all out yet. Point is, right now we stand a chance. So right now, the truth **HAS TO WAIT.**

At any rate, Vaguelandia will forever remain a mystery to the rest of us. Even from our **AERIAL VANTAGE POINT,** the secret realm is shrouded in fog and mist, making it impossible to decipher the shadowy forms below.

We seem to have attracted the **FULL** attention of Vaguelandia's top-notch land-to-air defense. Our dragon **SWERVES** as projectiles of various sizes and shapes fly at us from out of the mist below.

The dragon cradles us, turning his back to the ground as we await the **INEVITABLE.** The only thing I remember about our touchdown into Vaguelandia is that it was loud. **VERY** loud.

I awake to a dank and musty smell. It's dark.
I think I'm in some sort of dungeon, though
I'm not chained to anything. I'm lying on what
feels like a bed of **STRAW.** I sit up and pain
shoots across my temple. I touch the side f

my head and it's bandaged. Am I in some sort of moldy **HOSPITAL ROOM**? I will myself out of bed and stumble around the chamber.

DUDE, watch it!

trip

Terra and Gil seem okay, but I have no idea where Boulder and Ash are. We feel around the walls for an opening and find a tiny door that's really low to the ground. It's unlocked. I pull open the door, revealing a **CRAMPED TUNNEL** with light streaming in from the other end. Echoing down the passageway is what sounds like a bizarre mix of laughter and fighting. I crawl through the narrow shaft, emerging on the other side feeling both relief and even **MORE CONFUSION.**

I am super excited to see Boulder and Ash alive and at the center of some sort of... surprise party? Either that or they've been rounded up for **CEREMONIAL EXECUTION.** The creatures' giant axes and violent behavior make me uneasy. At the same time, the little guys are oddly cute and I want to pinch their cheeks. Gil and Terra soon trail into the room, and, judging by their faces, they too **SHARE** my bewilderment.

CHAPTER 21.

It's an honor, I guess, to be an honored guest. Definitely beats having my head lopped off, or whatever it is Vaguelandians do to unhonored things. Don't get me wrong, they seem nice and I keep wanting to pick them up and **SQUEEZE** them, but I restrain myself for fear that head-lopping might still be an option. So instead I just smile.

Luckily, they speak the common tongue. I can only imagine how much **WORSE** things would be if we couldn't understand each other. I ask the orbs what the big celebration is about, and from what I can gather, we're some sort of **HEROES.**

That's great! The Quest Kids are usually damaging villages, so it feels quite nice to finally have one **INDEBTED** to us. I have absolutely no clue what we did to deserve this, but I'm perfectly willing to be **CELEBRATED** for it.

We will eat like kings **FOREVER!**

YOU BETCHA!

So it looks like our celebration involves dinner. Not sure what this "forever" business is about, though. Overall, I'm still pretty **CLUELESS.** But before I get to puzzle over it any further, we're ushered from the party room into what looks to be Vaguelandia's town square. And it's then that everything finally starts to, kinda, sorta, make sense.

They're gonna **EAT OUR DRAGON**!

Well, not **OUR** dragon. Come to think of it, we barely know him. Though, in the span of the last twenty-four hours, he's saved us from questing peril twice! Yes, technically, we were only facing said peril to keep him from blazing up Bristolburg. But, still, I am **NOT** all right with this. And I calmly bring this up to our hosts.

Okay, maybe not so calmly. And there I go again, calling him **OUR** dragon. Why do I keep doing that? I mean, we did tell him he was our friend, but that was really so he would **RESCUE** and not **ROAST** us, right?

Either way, we're not standing by while these laughing lizard orbs feast upon our, kinda, sorta, **FRIEND.**

Well, that's a **RELIEF.** I feel kind of silly now for making a scene. Of course, it's not ideal that the dragon is still tied up in the middle of downtown. But, in their defense, this could be the only thing keeping him from vaporizing their village. Whatever the case, I'm back to having no idea why the little lizard orbs are so excited, and why **WE'RE** being so exalted.

Oh, right. They think we just rode a giant **FIRE MONSTER** into town for them to blast their BBQ with.

Looks like lizard orbs like their dinners ultra well-done. And more specifically, the kind of extra crispiness only afforded by a proper **DRAGON-BASED** flambé.

COOKING dinner definitely beats being COOKED for dinner, I always say. However, the dragon is less thrilled over being anointed the orbs' "forever" flame broiler. I try to address these concerns with the orbs, but once again become distracted by all of the SHARP POINTY THINGS surrounding us and I chicken out.

Vaguelandian tempers are unpredictable at best. Which means that to stay in their good graces, and in turn, ALIVE, the Quest Kids will do just what honored guests do when they're invited to dinner.

We will dine.

Dragon Barbecue:

A GUIDE TO VAGUELANDIAN CUISINE

TRANSLATED *and* RESTORED *by* J.B. LÜCASTOOTHÉ

L ittle may be known of the land and peoples of Vaguelandia, but thanks to Ned and the Quest Kids we now know of Vaguelandia's affinity for **DRAGON-ROASTED** meats. In doing further research of my own, I came across a brief excerpt from a 100 percent culturally **AUTHENTIC** Vaguelandian cookbook. So in classic Lücastoothé fashion (as one has grown accustomed), each recipe has been painstakingly restored and translated so as to satisfy your culinary curiosity. Please enjoy or, should I say, **BON APPÉTIT**!

Flaming Fowl

·—· Get a bird

—· Blast bird with **DRAGON FIRE**

·—· Try not to burn face off

Meat Helmet

- Take off helmet

- Fill helmet with meat

- Blast helmet with **DRAGON FiRE**

- Eat meat, not helmet

Death Nuggets

- Chop meat into nuggets

- Soak nuggets in **YOO BETCHA** sauce

- Blast nuggets with **DRAGON FiRE**

← SOOPAH HOT!!!

Smokin Stick Steak

- Find a stick

- Put steak on stick

- Scorch stick over open **DRAGON FiRE** (end with steak on it)

Meat-Wrapped Meaty Chunks

- Cut meat into chunks (**NOT** nuggets)

- Wrap meaty chunks with meat

- Char meaty chunks with **DRAGON FiRE**

MEAT.   MORE MEAT

CHAPTER 22

We're led across the village square and seated at the Vaguelandians' **TABLE OF HONOR.** But what they don't know is that the Quest Kids will not be eating. We have a plan. Okay, we don't **REALLY** have a plan. But we **WILL** have a plan. And maybe one before Boulder is even finished ordering. Being our own personal chef, Boulder knows a bit about food and often takes his own sweet time mulling over menus.

Cuz it doesn't work like that. It's a **MEMORY** spell. It can only teleport you to places you've been to before.

Oh.

That, and my teacher told me that the **EASY** ones can have side effects.

Side effects?

First one listed is **DEATH**. Then there's some other pretty horrible stuff. Hmm, what's **MELTY-GOO-BRAIN**?

But it's easy, right? We can just **TELEPORT** everybody back to the Bristolburg?

Maybe, but the easy spells can be **DECEIVING**.

How so?

Like, if you don't perform the easy ones just perfectly, magic punishes you more **HARSHLY**.

233

Gil seems reluctant, and even though he **WAS** able to summon a giant bird, well, dragon, I still don't have the utmost confidence in his spell-casting. Plus, the bird spell offered not nearly as much in the way of **DYING** or having our brains **MELTY-GOO'D.** The thoughts of which now send me nervously hiding behind my menu.

And it's then that I actually start reading the menu. It's all **MEAT.** Not one **VEGETABLE** listed. Do Vaguelandians even know what a vegetable is? Probably not. They've probably never farmed a day in their lives. But, wait! I have.

A plan quickly forms in my yet-to-be-melty-goo'd mind. And maybe it's the real **FEAR** that we're actually considering Gil's brain scramble, spell, but I find myself bypassing my friends' approval altogether and heading straight into me just **BLURTING** something out again.

Attention, Vaguelandia! You no longer have need of this **DRAGON!**

For I can show you a **BETTER** way!

What are you doing?!

It's okay, I have a **PLAN.**

I am a very **POWERFUL** farmer and I will now teach your people the ways of the vegetable!

I thought you said he was a **TERRIBLE** farmer.

He is.

I desperately scan the town square for a hoe or rake or anything that'll move dirt around so I can continue my demonstration. But, of course, **NO ONE** in Vaguelandia farms, so why would they have any of those things? Then I spy something that might just do the trick.

236

The lizard orbs angrily rush me. And after ducking their first couple axe blows, it becomes quite apparent that they're just not all that into agriculture. Had I known this earlier, I gladly would have gone with the melty-goo-brain option. Beats having my brain **LOPPED FREELY** from my body, right?

I flash an apologetic look to my friends. I really am sorry for having just instantly used up the last of our Vaguelandian goodwill. They look back in **HORROR** and get up to help, but I know they'll never reach me in time. 💀

Then, from nowhere, a lone lizard orb cries out.

Everyone's attention follows the direction of the orb's frantic **FINGER POINT**, which lands us squarely on the dragon. Only this time the dragon appears a little less tied down.

As Ash is **FLUNG ABOUT** this way and that by the dragon's tail, I can't help but smile. I never know how much our little pig-dog-thing understands about what's going on. But, apparently, while we'd all sat down to devise a plan to save our new friend, Ash just took it upon himself to, well, start saving.

The lizard orbs quickly cast me aside for the commotion being caused by Ash. Not only is the little guy single-handedly saving the dragon, but he's also **SAVING ME.** Now it's time for the rest of the Quest Kids to partake in our pig-dog-thing's plan already in progress.

CHAPTER 23

Ash's plan really isn't all that bad. It's simple, direct, and if we **CUT THROUGH** enough ropes before getting chopped, lopped, or **SKEWERED** ourselves, we'll be home free. It's the bold kind of plan we never would have attempted on our own, but now that we're here, we're really committing to it.

The lizard orbs run for their lives. It's a lot easier to tie down an **UNCONSCIOUS** dragon than to reckon with a very alert and angry one.

Not ideal, but I guess we can always run out of town. I don't know how keen the lizard orbs will be to chase after us. And I'd like to avoid Gil's easy but **HIGHLY LETHAL** teleportation spell, if at all possible. I still don't want to discover just how unpleasant "melty-goo-brain" can be.

The dragon looks down at us, slightly puzzled, and then cracks a smile. A tear starts pooling under one of his eyes. He leans down to my level, resting is face directly in front of mine. I won't lie, it's very **UNNERVING.** I've never been this close to a dragon's mouth before.

I think I kind of knew that already. After being saved, I figured the dragon might decide to reexamine his **FIERY PLAN** for mass destruction. But I guess I just didn't want to assume. Also, part of me really wants to finish this quest! I don't want to fail again.

C'mon, you'd look silly in just sweatpants. You **NEED** a super-sweet zip-up golden track jacket to go with them.

So be it. Let's go **SHAVE** some rage beast!

We start running out of town, in the direction of our **FINAL GOAL.** It felt good to know we weren't going to give up. It also felt good knowing that we wouldn't have to face the golden-fleeced rage beast alone.

As we run down Vaguelandia's main boulevard, we can see **NO TRACE** of the lizard orbs. This might provide me some relief if it wasn't for the faint noise of **CHANTING** in the air. And the more we run, the less faint it becomes.

The lizard orbs are obviously heavily armed enough to blow a dragon out of the sky, so sticking around to find out what **SAD MISFORTUNE** a "BRR-GANK" might bring us doesn't sound like too much fun. But in turning the corner, we soon discover that a "BRR-GANK" isn't a weapon at all.

It's way, way worse.

CHAPTER 24

'm not sure how the lizard orbs obtained their own golden-fleeced **RAGE BEAST.** With Vaguelandia being so close to the monster, maybe it was just a matter of time before their worlds collided. But it does not seem like an altogether healthy relationship. Certainly not like the dragon's and ours. Part of me even feels kind of sorry for the beast...nothing should be

chained up like that. But an even bigger part
of me is very thankful that it is.

Oh well, so much for that.

I don't know if you've ever had the pleasure
of being **CHARGED AT** by an unchained rage
beast, but let me tell you that if I'd been
able to move, I don't think it would have
done much good.

Thankfully, the dragon takes the brunt of that blow. I mean, that sucks for the dragon, but if we'd received a direct hit, this really would have been our **FINAL** quest attempt.

The dragon lies unconscious in what I think used to be some lizard orb's home. At least I hope he's just unconscious and not, you know...worse. The rage beast stands in the middle of town intently focused on the dragon it just **BARRELED** into.

Meanwhile, my friends and I are in shock and in **UTTER DISBELIEF** that our recently freed and **MASSIVELY HUGE** dragon friend could be defeated so quickly. We're more than a little unsure about what to do next.

Sure, instant death and brain goo are not ideal, but they seem like way better fates than being **PULVERIZED** by a rage beast. Plus, we have no time to think of anything else. So I quickly remind my friends what the mystic told me.

Then we should stay and **FIGHT!**

What?!

The mystic said we'd **TRIUMPH** over a beast of gold.

Teleporting is **NOT** being triumphant. It's running away!

Terra, stop...

Ned's mystic got us this far. Trust in her and all will **WORK OUT!**

258

That's what this is about? So you can show your mom and dad you're a **REAL** quester? Ned, they're not here!

Yeah, but **WE** are, and **YOU** lied to us.

(accusatory glares)

They're right. I lied to the people I care about the most...the ones who haven't abandoned me. And it wasn't some little "cat-dangle" of a lie. It was a huge monstrous beast of a lie, told for the wrong reasons, that could ultimately get them killed. I am a **NOT** a good friend.

CHAPTER 25

O kay, I admit, I felt pretty heroic making my big selfless gesture to save our new friend. But that feeling lasts about two seconds, after which Gil promptly informs me that for **ALL** intended teleportees to teleport to safety, they need to be **TOUCHING.** Which means we'll need to run past a **CURRENTLY RAGING** rage beast and into a pile of rubble to hold hands with a hopefully not-dead dragon.

Fortunately or unfortunately, depending on how you look at it, there's still no time for a better plan, so we commence darting into downtown Vaguelandia. Luckily, the rage beast pays little notice to our group scurrying by, preferring instead to **PACE** and **SNORT** in anticipation of its adversary popping back up.

We soon see that the dragon is still very much unconscious, or, you know, worse. I guess we'll find out which it is **AFTER** we teleport. That is if we **ALL** don't end up worse than unconscious, too. We grab hold of each other's hands and I touch the dragon's leg. Gil opens his book to deliver the spell, but freezes when he notices something a little off.

It seems **NOT EVERY** lizard orb was clued in on the dragon's escape. This one had just sat down to enjoy his extremely baked BBQ only to have his lovely home and dinner table flattened by the cook. The poor Vaguelandian appears to be in shock. Until our impromptu entry revives him.

Gil opens his book to the teleportation spell and tracks his finger down the page. I look out of what used to be the front of this lizard orb's home and see the rage beast fixated in **OUR** direction.

I look again and see the rage beast charging. The **GROUND SHAKES** each time a giant foot slams down against it. Then the beast's feet leave the ground entirely as it jumps straight into the air. I can only assume that its next destination is down on us.

CHAPTER 26

My brain hurts. Though it doesn't feel like it's melty-gooing out of my nose, so that's a **PLUS.** I look over to my right. We appear to be in a village, but not the lizard orbs' village. It's Ifer's village. Bristolburg. But for some reason everyone seems to be running, crying, and/or screaming. Then I turn my head to the left and see why.

So much for saving the village. If it's any consolation, it looks like the rage beast part of whatever I'm looking at is doing **MOST** of the damage. And really, we only ever promised to save them from an angry fire-breathing dragon.

I'm pretty **ZONKED** from being teleported, but I force myself to sit up and call for my friends. Gil more precisely. Not that it does us much good now, but I'd like to know what happened.

GIL! What's going on?!

Whoopsie.

WHOOPSIE?! Gil explains that further down the list of side effects for the spell is something called "form-fusion." Apparently, when two or more things are teleported at the same time, sometimes they can get jumbled up. This pretty much answers what happened to the rage beast and the dragon, and, well, us...

This is better than being dead, right?

Sure, it's cliché to say that this quest brought us **CLOSER** together, but that's the literal truth. I'd never heard of form-fusion before today. I never even knew it was a possibility, but this is my reality now. Forever merged with my best friends! Only they're not all that happy about it.

As much as I'd like to honor Boulder's request, I'm afraid that he's **STUCK** with us. Man, I gotta stop with the form-fusion puns! Gil points at the beastdragon **STOMPING** in our direction, which finally sparks Boulder to get up and move.

OPTION A: RUN

Needless to say, we have **NOT MASTERED** the fine art of running away as one giant Quest Kid with five different brains. Thankfully, the beastdragon is being slowed by its sleeping dragon side.

I don't have a quick answer for them. I don't know the ins and outs of form-fusion. But somehow, **WE** all retained our own minds, so maybe there's a chance the dragon did, too.

Very funny, Gil. Yes, at the start of all this, we simply wanted to make off with a sleeping dragon's golden sweatpants. Now we have to wake that same dragon to have any chance at survival. Ironic? Maybe. Alas, there's **NO TIME** for all that, so we just stay with Option A. But as you already know, Option A can also have side effects.

Boulder trips again, which is easy to understand, since what used to be a rock troll is now a mashed-potatoed-friend-monster. We go down **HARD.** This time, though, instead of being side-stepped by the giant-scary-thing chasing us, it trips on the hard-heavy-thing in its path.

CHAPTER 27

Now both sides of the beastdragon appear to be **KNOCKED OUT,** but I know this is only temporary. I still have no idea how to save Bristolburg. What's the matter with me? Why do I keep on dragging monsters back to villages?! It's like **QUEST ATTEMPT 2** over and over again!

I seem **DOOMED** to repeat the same mistakes, never really learning anything as I go along. I'm no quester, I'm just another monster standing before the ruins of another **FAILED QUEST.**

Only this quest isn't over yet.

The dragon is no longer fused with the golden-fleeced rage beast, and is now looking somewhat confused. He scans the village, taking in the **FULL MAGNITUDE** of destruction and chaos he appears to have caused. He's **HORRIFIED.**

I can only imagine what the dragon must be thinking, waking up to this mayhem and seeing this **NIGHTMARISH** cluster of his new friends. But it does make me wonder...why is he no longer nightmarishly clustered with the rage beast?

The **IMPACT** must have separated them.

It seems that form-fusion is only temporary, and the jolt of falling into that building jarred them loose. Which gives me hope, knowing that I'm only one **GIANT IMPACT** away from not being stuck like this forever! Maybe when all of this is done, we can get the dragon to drop-kick us. The perfect end to a perfect quest. But first we need to figure out what to do about the rage beast.

Then, from nowhere, we hear a familiar voice.

COUGH...sing it to sleep...**COUGH**...**COUGH**...

Followed by a familiar laugh.

As if our day couldn't get any more disturbing. I guess the lizard orb whose house we
crashed ended up teleporting along with us,
and is now...**TRYING** to help? The thing is, the
rage beast is already knocked out, so I don't
see how "singing it to sleep" is going to
make a difference. Which is what I bring
up to Boulder's backside.

The rage beast starts to **RUMBLE.** We don't have much time and I don't think it's going to be in the mood for a **MUSICAL NUMBER** when it wakes up. So then what do we do? Is it more of Option A, followed shortly thereafter by Option B?

I guess chains were somewhat effective for the lizard orbs that one time. You know, until the beast **COMPLETELY SNAPPED** them to pieces. But before I can even ask about Bristolburg's current shackle inventory, the dragon comes up with another familiar option.

CHAPTER 28

I admit, **OPTION D: TALK** did sort of work out for us the first go-round, but that's only because we knew the dragon could speak. This was abundantly clear from the moment he screamed at us for "disturbing his slumber." However, in our **CURRENT DILEMMA**, the rage beast has yet to utter a single phrase to make me think it'll respond well to a good talking-to.

Before the dragon can finish his sentence, with what I can only assume is the word "this," he's hit from behind, **HARD.** Being that we're all pretty much MMOR now, the collision doesn't hurt that much. But it does send everyone spiraling in opposite directions. Our forms, **UNFUSED.**

Luckily, I don't lose consciousness this time. The dragon, however, is once again knocked out cold. The golden-fleeced rage beast stares down Bristolburg's beaten boulevard, with its focus completely locked-in on the dragon. Then it starts whooping, and thumping its chest.

This isn't going to end well. Not at all like the mystic had envisioned. I mean, had there ever really been a mystic in the first place. We will **NOT** be triumphant this day. The rage beast will kill the dragon and then, in ever-so-effective rage-beast fashion, do away with the rest of us. It's time to get my friends to safety. I owe them that at least. But how? Then, out of the corner of my eye, I see a **COMFORTING SIGHT.**

Ifer waves to us from her storefront, gesturing to "move quickly!" We book it toward the bagelry, stopping just short of the entryway. I stand on the front porch and usher all my friends inside. But instead of going in behind them, I **SLAM** the heavy door closed.

I grab a chair from the front porch and wedge it up against the door. I have a plan.

Don't worry, this plan's **WAY BETTER** than my violently mobbed farming demo. At least, I hope so. I dart back to the center of town

and close in on the rage beast. It still
appears very much fixated on the dragon,
who continues his struggle to get upright.
The beast aggressively thumps its chest and
snarls. I approach cautiously, taking special
care not to disturb the beast's focus. It's
then that I fish around my belt for the one
item **PERFECTLY SUITED** to execute my plan.

I just shaved a rage beast! Mission accomplished, y'all! Well, sort of. I mean, I didn't shave the **ENTIRE** rage beast. I really only **CLIPPER'D** its bungus a little. But it's the farthest anyone has ever gotten. How cool is that?!

Don't worry. This isn't the entire plan. I mean, I'm not *going* to just traipse up behind a rage beast, shear its rear, and then wait to be beaten senseless. That was just **PHASE ONE: AGITATION.** I need the rage beast to be, well, enraged. I know that seems to be its resting state, but I need to give it good reason to leave our mutual dragon friend behind and stomp after me instead.

Which leads us to **PHASE TWO** of my plan.
And if you've been paying close attention to
this story, it should be pretty familiar.

Right, it gets confusing. **PHASE TWO** being
OPTION A? But try to keep up. Now that
I have the rage beast's full and undivided
attention, I am doing my darnedest to get
OUT of Bristolburg.

I know what you're thinking. Say I can actually
Option A my way out of town **BEFORE** the rage
beast ends up stomping me into compost. What's

to stop the beast from just heading right back into town to resume his previously scheduled rage-fest? At the end of the day, maybe I bought the village, like, **TWELVE SECONDS**???

Which brings us to **PHASE THREE** of my plan. Where is it that mountain villages reside again? Anyone? Anyone? That's right, in the mountains! And, as you may or may not remember, mountains are very tall, equipped with ledges and whatnot. Everyone see where I'm going with this?

well,
poo.

CHAPTER 29

This is awkward. I was really looking
forward to you seeing **PHASE FOUR.** The
one where I jump out of the way at the last
second and the rage beast **PLUMMETS** to its
death. Kinda the phase I was most proud of.
But instead, the rage beast just looks down
at me, with an expression that's not necessarily

all that ragey, but more like, "Hey, I just outsmarted you and I'm just the big scary rage beast." If I didn't know any better, I'd say the beast was **GLOATING.**

Rather than sticking around to be ridiculed, I put **PHASE FIVE** into action. I pivot ever-so-slightly to the left and start running toward the Halls of Wisdom, where, if I can keep this pace up for two weeks, the rage beast will be so let down by the Elves' lackluster library that it'll throw its **OWN SELF** off a cliff! Okay, so Phase Five might need some work, but before I even get to iron out the kinks, the beast grabs me.

Having exhausted **ALL PHASES**, it is now time for the golden-fleeced rage beast's plan. And whether that involves me simply being chucked over the edge of the cliff, or perhaps just ripped limb from limb, or maybe some limb-ripping followed by some edge-chucking, I don't know. Regardless, my life is **LITERALLY** in its hands. So I close my eyes and await whatever.

Only nothing happens. I'm still in midair, mind you, held aloft by a terrifying rage beast. But when I open my eyes, I see that the beast barely even notices me. Instead, it's looking skyward and moving its head this way and that, tracking some unknown target. Then the beast quickly lifts me up and uses me as a make-shift shield against the approaching thing. And it's then that I can finally see just what kind of a **THING** this thing is.

pig-dog-thing

I'm not really sure what's happening. I mean, the thing part of our favorite pig-dog-thing is probably dragon, as we learned earlier. And as we all know, dragons can fly. But dragons also have wings, and Ash **DOES NOT.** Plus, he's never ever flown before! Yet there he is, doing the very thing that he's not supposed to be able to do, and doing it pretty well, too.

As I'm being whipped around **WILLY-NILLY** like a kind of fly-swatter, I start to black out. Sure was nice seeing Ash, though. Heck, it was nice seeing anyone! I'd fully expected to be dead by now. Oh well, that probably comes next.

But in betwixt swattings, I regain a little consciousness and look down. And then I notice Terra. Hey, Terra! Her bow is expertly drawn back with an arrow aimed right at me. I think she must still be mad at me for lying. That, or she's pity-arrowing me before the rage beast can shake my **HEAD LOOSE.** Either way, it sure was nice seeing her, too.

I can only assume that she meant to hit the
rage beast's hand, because Terra **DOESN'T
MISS.** It loosens the beast's grip in the midst
of a good whipping and I'm released skyward.
I don't know if that's because I'm so light-
headed from lack of blood flow to my brain,
but time slows for a minute, and it feels quite
splendid to be up here floating in space.

Then I hit the ground, and that feels, well, less splendid. Luckily, I managed to land on the right side of the cliff, meaning the side **NOT LOCATED** at the bottom of a rocky gorge. I shake off the cobwebs and look up at Terra, who's pulling out another arrow from her quiver. The rage beast winces while examining its wound and then glares at the one-eyed elf who put it there.

I thought we all agreed **NOT** to go this way.

I did almost lead my friends off **THIS** very cliff at the beginning of our quest. Now here they are, pulling me back from the edge again. The only question is, **HOW** are they doing this? I locked them in Ifer's shop! Well, one of them is MMOR, so it probably wasn't too hard to bust out of there.

See? The door opens **INWARD**.

creak

Speaking of, I look directly behind the beast and there's Boulder. He smiles and raises a "shh" finger.

The beast pulls the arrow from his new **HAND PIERCING** and appears ready to trample me and Terra. I look back at her to say *goodbye*, but she looks right past me and then nods. I turn and see Gil about twenty feet away. He nods back, chanting and holding his wizard staff high in the air. Then he starts lowering the staff, and, as he does so, Ash begins floating down. Gil then rotates the staff in a circular motion, and Ash follows a similar path. The end result of all of this is Ash's **REAR END** pointing directly at the rage beast's face.

I'm not entirely sure what "phase" my friends' plan is entering now, but it does appear to be the **FINAL** one. And not to get too nit-picky about it, but I do have concerns over the **ECOLOGICAL IMPACT** of this phase, not to mention its impact on us. But before I get to lodge a formal complaint, I get tackled.

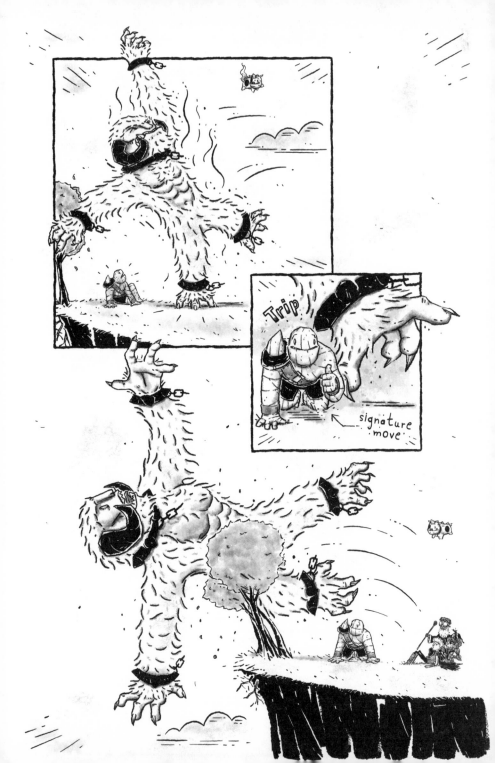

None of us can believe it. Someway, somehow,
we **TRIUMPHED** over a beast of gold. And it
took each and every one of us to make it
happen. We start laughing. I wave my hand in
front my nose, and we all look over at Ash. I
don't think anything will ever grow here again.

tree
roots →

The rage beast climbs up over the edge and
somehow appears even more full of rage. The
relief on our faces turns to resignation. We
gave it our **BEST SHOT**, and the beast still
didn't go down. My friends and I look at each
other once again, and we hold hands, Knowing
it'll be the **LAST THING** we ever do.

After waiting for the average time it takes for a beast to **OBLITERATE** a questing quintet, I still feel Boulder's and Terra's hands clutching my own. So I open my eyes just to confirm I'm not, like, holding two **UNBODIED** arms. Thankfully, everyone's appendages are still attached. And then I look up at the rage beast, who's not even looking at us. It's looking **OVER** us.

Well, this is promising. Granted, the rage beast made quick work of the dragon during their last couple of run-ins, but there's something **DIFFERENT** about the dragon this time. I can't quite put my finger on it, but for some reason I'm not worried.

Okay, maybe I'm **A LITTLE** worried. Had the beast's last blow unlocked something in the dragon? After the form-fusion, was there more beast brain in there than dragon? Who knows? All I know is that we're still holding hands and it's starting to feel a little weird. Cuz, like, how long is **TOO LONG**, you know?

So we just continue to stand there, hand in hand, stuck between the dragon and the rage beast. Suddenly, the beast's expression begins to soften. Its breath becomes more controlled. Its rage starts to...**SUBSIDE**? And the dragon, no longer pounding his chest, slowly approaches the beast, gently chuffing and ever-so-softly snorting.

We back out of the way and finally let go of each other. Then we realize what's going on. The dragon is doing exactly what he said he'd do. He's talking to the rage beast. And he's doing it in the beast's **OWN LANGUAGE.**

As the dragon closes in, I look behind him and see a crowd of Bristolburgians assembling at the edge of town. Everyone is gathering to bear witness to the **FINAL CONFRONTATION**, but discovering something so much better in its place.

It **WAS** sort of beautiful. **TWO TITANS** not tearing at each other or stomping on any of us, just peacefully communicating. Who knows? Maybe being fused together had, in fact, given them a new and **BIZARRE** understanding. Either way, the dragon and the rage beast are really making a strong connection.

The dragon turns back toward Bristolburg
and explains to its citizens what he just told
the rage beast. Something about how he knew
what it was like to be **MISUNDERSTOOD.** To be
branded a monster.

The dragon continues on, saying that letting
go of his anger and forgiving others was his
pathway to learning to love again. Or something
like that. It was kind of a **LONG SPEECH** and
I was super out of it from almost being killed
like eight times. But when it was all over,
everyone felt pretty emotional.

The day ends with another thing I thought
I'd never see. A dragon and a beast and
a village full of people coming **TOGETHER**.
And not in a weird, form-fused kind of way,
but in a way where everyone finally kind of
understands one another.

I look over at my friends and feel like we have a better understanding, too. They know that I would do **ANYTHING** for them. And I know now that they will **ALWAYS** have my back.

In the end, I was **SUPER RIGHT** about everything working out. I mean, not to get too technical about it or anything, but I didn't need a mystic to tell me that my friends and I were capable of amazing things. I totally knew that already :)

QUEST SUCCESS #1: TOLD YOU SO

scribble
scribble

CHAPTER 30

Well, we've come to the end of our first field guide, and hopefully you've learned something along the way. I admit, the Quest Kids aren't perfect. We make **TONS** of mistakes. But you know what? That's how we get better. So whatever you do, don't let **OUR** mistakes stop you from getting out there and making some mistakes of your own. That way **YOU** can get better.

Where do we go from here? Who knows? I do know that our new dragon friend is a whole lot happier. And, apparently, he had **A NAME** this entire time. Which I feel guilty for not asking about much earlier, especially since the rage beast and lizard orbs seem to have been on a first-name basis.

Golden Goliaths

BRR-GANK as
"THE GOLDEN-FLEECED
RAGE BEAST"

TREVOR as
"THE DRAGON WITH
THE PANTS OF GOLD"

Trevor never did get his track jacket, but he did get a roommate. He and Brr-gank hit it off and are now **INSEPARABLE!** Well, a little more separable than when they were form-fused, but still.

As far as Bristolburg goes, the villagers are rebuilding and we're all pitching in. For the very first time, we'll be leaving a village in **BETTER SHAPE** than when we found it.

Even the lizard orb who hitched a ride on Boulder's backside has learned the error of his ways and is picking up a few new techniques to **SHARE** with his own village back home.

320

And in return, the lizard orb is teaching the villagers what **HE KNOWS.**

We even run into Ifer again, and she presents us with our very own **VICTORY** bagels.

As for our next chapter, it remains unwritten. After six failed quest attempts and us finally achieving some success, it looks as though we've become **PROFESSIONAL** questers now.

There's a feeling of satisfaction, knowing the job's complete, but also a bit of sadness, knowing that it's time to move on.

Ready to go?

Almost. Just one more thing.

step

I want you to have this.

A **RiNG**?

NOT a ring! Definitely **NOT** a ring!

Then what is it?

A piece of the rage beast's **FLEECE** that I snipped off.

I took it to a seamstress in town.

And she helped me make it into **THIS**.

A **HAIR TIE** for your ponytail.

Ohhh...

An elf started questing for this all those years ago. Now that we're done, maybe a piece of it should end up with an elf, too.

Then on behalf of the **ELVES**, we thank you.

foster

Grandma's, grandma's, grandma's...

And I want to thank **ALL** of you.

For sticking by me, even though, um, I lied and stuff. And just so you know, no more cat-dangling, like, **EVER.**

Because **FRIENDSHIPS** are built on trust.

And you are my **BEST** friends.

The truth is, I don't need to lie anymore. Having just accomplished something that the most accomplished elf in the world could not, we've finally found our confidence. Now we can turn the page and get back to the real reasons we went out questing in the first place.

I miss them. And I may never know if their disappearance had anything to do with me. But I do know that I **WANT** to find them. Not only that, I'm ready to. It's clear to me now that this field guide isn't just for you. It's also for them. So they can one day see that **THIS** is me. This is who I really am. I'm a quester.

Deep down, I've always known who I was. I've never needed a book to convince me of it. And whether my parents should come to believe it or not is on them. But in a world where dragons and rage beasts can end up seeing eye to eye, maybe there's a real chance for the rest of us.

Don't suppose anyone knows where we're going...

Afterword

I hope you were just as illuminated by this book as I was after recovering it from those dark subterranean caverns so many years ago. Lucky for you, loyal reader, there are a great **MANY MORE** quests that I am currently restoring for your enjoyment in the years to come.

Perhaps, like me, you drew a bit of inspiration and maybe learned a life lesson or two from young Ned and his band of Questing Kids. Personally, my favorite part was when everyone was form-fused together. It made me wonder what that might be like.

Perhaps science, which is the magic of today, will someday illuminate this for us all.

–'Til our next adventure!

J.B. Lucastoothe

P.S. – *Enclosed with this edition* is an excerpt taken from a **TATTERED PARCHMENT** I excavated from deep inside the Carpathian Mountains near Moldova. Though it seemed indecipherable at first, I have pieced together an entry that may be of importance.

We have moved swiftly for three days and nights, making our way to the land of the Elves. We're told that ancient wisdom resides there which could prove potent against the shadow now cast upon us. In desperation, we leave our only son behind. For the journey ahead is steeped in peril, worsened still by the looming darkness spurring us on. Our hastened departure provides some hope that what we hold most dear will be kept safe.

Let the Elves' storied "Halls" be just as glorious as proclaimed. We may need every bit of their powerful "Wisdom" to deliver us from this terrible evil. At least, so says our guide, Gazimar...

Acknowledgements

Lücastoothé Enterprises, Inc. would like to recognize the following family, friends and/or ferrets for their roles in helping us shape this book into being...

Lisa, Lucy, Brody, Josie, Jean, Richard, John, Rob, Jen, Geri, Noree, Mary, Bernard, (other) John, David, Sarah, Dan, (other other) John, Mary Jo, Andrew, Jason, Mike, Fred, Monty, and Oscar.

Other non-ferreted parties who were **CRUCIAL** to the formation of this book include...

Stephen and Erica with Writers House. Thank you for your tireless efforts in helping us excavate Ned's manuscript so that it might finally see the light of day.

Tracey, Chris, Whitney, Melissa, Rich, Marcie and the rest of the Union Square Kids crew. Thank you for your guidance in this book's final restoration and providing a path with which to bring it to the world.

A last bit of recognition goes out to those of whom we do not know, but without their inspiration, this book just would not be: Bill, Berkeley, Jeff, Dav, Raina, and J.R.R.

About J.B. Lücastoothé

Renowned children's book archaeologist and ferret enthusiast J.B. Lücastoothé happily resides in northern England.

He has twenty-four ferrets.

Well, he actually has twenty-five, but at the time of this writing one is missing.

J.B. is pretty sure that that's the one that took his car keys.

In unrelated news, J.B.'s car is missing.

Note: *If anyone sees a ferret driving a lime-green 1984 Pontiac Fiero GT with license plate FRIT-4-LIF, please contact J.B. straightaway!*

About Mark Leiknes

When he's not serving as the live-in
Cartoonist/Ferret Events Coordinator for
Lücastoothé Enterprises Inc., Mark Leiknes
normally resides in northern America with
his wife and three children.

Over the years, Mark has proven to be
an important part of J.B.'s book restoration
process. But what's even more important is
that Mark's contract specifically states that
he's to "keep the car keys hidden away from
twenty-five genius-level ferrets at ALL TIMES."

The contract is way super clear about that.
Like, for real.

In unrelated news, Mark loves his family,
and will be coming home very soon.